Reviews

"Amid the turbulence of the times, Cantwell accurately integrates the development of Mexico in the 1500s with a storyline that decries prejudice and supports freedom and dignity for all. Cantwell describes, in vivid detail, the sights, sounds, and aromas of the fabled city of Tenochtitlan. 'Who is my real father?' Peter Collins learns the answer to this haunting question in the conclusion of this, the third book of the Tollan Trilogy, THE HALLS OF MONTEZUMA."

—Marie La France
EC Programs for Young Children
Massachusetts Department of Education

"I would recommend this book to adventure lovers of all ages."

—Susan DiRaimo
English Department
City College of New York

Praise for Book One, THE SECRET OF THE SMOKING MIRROR, awarded Editor's Choice for fiction.

"A fantastic tale about two children who travel back in time to ancient Mexico to save a civilization from destruction within. Fantasy, history, and an adventure that should be remembered for valor triumphing over evil with the aid of the future's science and the guiding spirit of Quetzalcoatl, who still stands watch over those who place trust in him."

—Claudia Dias
Writer, modavivendi.com

The Halls of Montezuma

The Halls of Montezuma

Book Three of the Tollan Trilogy

Michael Cantwell

iUniverse, Inc.
Bloomington

The Halls of Montezuma
Book Three of the Tollan Trilogy

iUniverse books may be ordered through booksellers or by contacting:

iUniverse
1663 Liberty Drive
Bloomington, IN 47403
www.iuniverse.com
1-800-Authors (1-800-288-4677)

ISBN: 978-1-4759-5847-8 (sc)
ISBN: 978-1-4759-5849-2 (hc)
ISBN: 978-1-4759-5848-5 (e)

Library of Congress Control Number: 2012920224

Printed in the United States of America

iUniverse rev. date: 11/30/2012

Dedication

Once again, to the memory of my father and mother

and for my sister, Anne-Marie

Acknowledgments

Several sources were invaluable to me in my research for this novel. Chief among them were *Cortéz & Montezuma* by Maurice Collis, *The Conquest of New Spain* by Diaz del Castillo, and *Quetzalcoatl and the Irony of Empire* by David Carrasco.

LIST OF MAJOR CHARACTERS

Peter Collins—Teenage time traveler born in twentieth-century America.

Rosa Guzman—Peter's classmate and companion in his time travels.

Quetzalcoatl—The plumed serpent, god of life and wisdom.

Tezcalipoca (Smoking Mirror)—God of war and death.

Quetzalcoatl Topiltzin—Tenth-century king of Tollan II who becomes the incarnation of Quetzalcoatl. He is driven out of Mexico and vows to reclaim his throne in five hundred years.

Montezuma—Emperor of the Aztec Empire at the time of the Spanish invasion.

Hernan Cortés—Spanish conquistador whom Montezuma and others believe is Quetzalcoatl Topiltzin returning to reclaim his throne.

Luis Alvarado—Aide to Cortés who becomes commander of Cholula in 1530 and bans marriage between Spanish troops and Native Americans.

Lieutenant Francisco Juarez—Spanish soldier who marries a Native American woman.

Sulma Juarez—His beloved wife.

Louise Collins—Peter's mother.

Ben—Peter's stepfather.

PART I

Chapter 1

⌒⌒

W*as it all a dream?* Peter Collins, teaching himself to shave, looked hard in the mirror and wondered. It had been two years since he'd traveled in time to ancient Mexico—that is, if it hadn't been just a dream. Yet, dream or no dream, those travels had changed his life. He was no longer a nerd, a wimp shunned by his schoolmates. He was captain of his high school freshman soccer team, getting good grades in his classes, and making friends.

Yet, aside from the question of whether it all had been a dream, two questions continued to haunt him. First, if all those things that had happened to him and Rosa in ancient Mexico had indeed been real, why hadn't Quetzalcoatl, the plumed serpent who had guided them through their time travels, returned as he had promised? It had been two years ago today, at the appearance of the morning star, that Quetzalcoatl had last come for them. Whenever the planet Venus appeared as the morning star, Peter was out of bed, looking through his telescope, hoping to see a sign of the flying serpent flitting across the moon and skidding down a ray of starlight aimed at Peter's bedroom window.

And the big question, the one that had gnawed at Peter's heart for as long as he could remember, the question that had led him to take his chances with Quetzalcoatl in the first place, remained unanswered. Who was his real father? Peter would be fourteen tomorrow, and he still didn't know. His mother had yet to tell him, and the serpent had given no hints. Okay, the serpent had said the secret would be revealed after Peter passed all three tests laid out for him. Well, he had passed two of them. On their first visit to ancient Mexico, he had solved the secret of the Smoking Mirror, thereby defeating the evil lords of Tollan I. On their next trip, six weeks later, he'd won the sacred ball game in Tollan II. Rosa passed her tests, bringing her the confidence and the respect of fellow students in school. One test remained. Peter was eager to take it, but he'd been waiting two years.

Standing now in front of his bathroom mirror, Peter thought about how he and Rosa had discussed their adventures in ancient Mexico together many times and in great detail, Rosa sometimes reminding him of things he'd forgotten. If their time travels had happened only in dreams, it was hard to believe they had just happened to have the same dreams. But how did you explain two years with no sign of Quetzalcoatl?

With all these questions hanging over his head, Peter went downstairs for breakfast. He found his mother sitting at the kitchen table, sipping coffee and smiling up at him. Yes, she was still as beautiful as the great goddess of Tollan I.

"Good morning, birthday boy," she said. "You'll be fourteen years old at exactly five-thirty tomorrow morning. What a lovely young man you are growing up to be! I'm so proud of you!" She got up to pour coffee into his waiting cup. His breakfast of sliced fruit and yogurt was set beside it. "Yes, tomorrow will be a big day," she went on. "I have a big surprise for you—something very special just for your birthday."

Peter was stunned. Something special just for his birthday? Was she going to tell him who his real father was at last? He had never summoned the courage to ask her straight-out, fearing it might embarrass her. But she had to know it was on his mind.

His mother sat down, folding her hands over her stomach and smiling. "Ben is coming home tomorrow!"

"Ben?" Peter shuddered.

"Yes, Ben is coming home from the mental asylum. He's coming home for good. Isn't that wonderful?"

"Wonderful?" Peter wanted to cry out in protest. But he knew his mother would be offended. One of the reasons he'd been feeling better about himself lately was that his stepfather had been away. He'd been a patient in Back to Reality Hospital for two years. It was Ben who had made him feel so bad about himself, telling him time and time again that he was a wimp, afraid of his own shadow, not made of the right stuff. And it was Ben who had wanted Peter put away in the hospital.

His wife had agreed on the condition that the whole family would be given examinations. As it turned out, Peter had passed his with flying colors while Ben had been found to be in dire need of mental treatment. Having been exposed to her husband's wild mood swings, Peter's mother had signed a paper to have him put away. Peter knew she was unhappy about it and feared that Ben would never recover and that the home life she'd once shared with him was gone forever. Not that it had been much of a happy home life the last few years. But looking back, it seemed to Peter his mother's marriage with Ben had been a fairly good one years ago. The trouble really had begun with his own coming of age, the problems he had started to have at school, trying to grow up—problems that had led Ben to decide he wasn't born with the right stuff.

Whatever the cause, Peter dreaded the thought of having to live with Ben again. Whenever his mother dragged Peter to the hospital on visiting days, he was exposed to the same old insults. Luckily, he had avoided going to the hospital for over six months now, inventing one excuse or another: soccer practice, special events. No, he couldn't live with Ben again, even to please his mother.

His only hope lay in a potential birthday present from Quetzalcoatl, a visit in the morning. Last time, Rosa had received a sign of his coming. He decided to ask her if she knew anything.

Chapter 2

◠

Peter and Rosa were both in high school now. Although they were still friends, they no longer shared classes. In fact, recently, Peter had found himself avoiding her again. Back in middle school, Rosa had been a skinny, obnoxious pain in the butt. She had been a sourpuss most of the time and hadn't been able to get through a single day without arguing with somebody. But now, Rosa was in possession of poise and confidence. And she was doing well in her classes. All these things won her the approval of teachers and fellow students.

And she had blossomed physically as well. Her figure was filling out with curves that made Peter's heart turn upside down whenever they met. He could not understand the new feelings he was having for her and had no control over them.

For this reason, he found himself avoiding her more often than he had when she was a mere pain in the butt. So it was with mixed feelings that he approached her now in the schoolyard.

"Rosa, I need to talk to you," he said.

"I think I know why." Rosa smiled her stunning smile. Then it struck Peter. Her smile was more evidence that it couldn't have been all just a dream. Her front teeth had been crooked until two years ago when a quetzal bird had straightened them for her. No one received dental work in dreams.

"Rosa, I find myself wondering—"

"Peter, I have news for you. A little bird came to visit me last night, the same bird who straightened my teeth. 'Pack your things,' he told me. 'Quetzalcoatl, the feathered serpent, needs you. Big things are happening in old Mexico, things that will change the world forever. He wants you to help him set things right. Be ready when the morning star arrives tomorrow. It should appear in the sky just before dawn.' So get ready, Peter. And by the way, happy birthday!"

Chapter 3

~

When Peter woke up the next morning, rays of light were streaming through his window. The clock on his dresser read five o'clock. He knew the sun wasn't expected to rise until seven. Peter jumped out of bed and looked out the window. There it was: Venus, the morning star, ablaze in the night sky. Then he saw the feathered serpent flying over the old pear tree in his yard. Rosa was sitting on his back, holding tight to the feathered coat as she bounced up and down. Her dark hair was braided. She wore a Mexican embroidered blouse and tan shorts. Peter stepped back as girl and serpent sailed through the window without breaking any glass. They landed next to Peter's desk. The god Quetzalcoatl, in his snakelike form, sat on his coils. His head almost touched the ceiling. Stretched from head to tail, he was at least sixteen feet long. Rosa slid off the feathered coat and laughed while Peter looked on, trembling with anticipation. He was also a little chilly and threw on an overshirt. He was otherwise dressed in a T-shirt and shorts. He only needed to slip on his sneakers.

"Good morning, sleepyhead." Rosa beamed.

Quetzalcoatl smiled, baring his fangs and fixing his bottle-green eyes on Peter. "Are you ready for your big test, Peter?"

"Yes, I'm packed and all set to go," he exclaimed, pulling his knapsack over his shoulders. "Where in space-time are we going on this trip?"

The serpent's expression turned serious as he knitted his brow in thought. "In many ways, this is the most dangerous mission I will have sent you on. And the most important. You are going to a time and place where great civilizations are about to clash. The gods themselves are at war with one another. The future of Mexico and of all the world depends on the outcome. You must play your part in preventing catastrophe. Are you ready?"

"At your service," Peter said. Rosa smiled and nodded in agreement.

"I'm sending you to the city of the Aztecs, Tenochtitlan. It was once the greatest and most beautiful city in the world. Yet it was to become the scene of the greatest violence the world had ever known. The mission I'm sending you on is actually two missions, but they are tied together. If you want to back out, I won't blame you. What do you say?"

"I say let's go," Peter said.

"You know I want to go," Rosa said.

"Very well." The serpent smiled, showing his clawlike fangs. "You met Topiltzin on your last trip. As you discovered, he was my incarnation in Tollan II. You saw him leave Mexico in disgrace, embarking on a raft of snakes into what is now known as the Gulf of Mexico. And just as the raft rose from the sea in a blaze of light, you heard him announce that he would return in one coil of time to reclaim his throne. A coil of time is five hundred years as I have told you. When you arrive in Mexico, it will be the year 1519, just about the time Quetzalcoatl was to return according to prophecy. So are we ready?"

"Let's get started," Rosa and Peter assented.

"All right, then. Take this feather from my coat, the one that just lit up. As you know, my feathered suit is a genetic code of all space-time. Take the feather, hold hands, close your eyes, and off you go!"

Chapter 4

~

The room shook violently, and suddenly the children found themselves racing through a blur of space-time. At last, streaks of all colors resolved themselves into a starlit sky. Then the stars were gone, and the sun appeared in a blue morning sky. An embankment of clouds lay below them. As they descended, the children caught their first glimpse of the famous Aztec city. Now they were falling at terrifying speeds, faster and faster with each passing second.

"Open your feathered parachute, quick," Peter called out to Rosa. They pulled the parachutes that had been given to them on their first trip out of their knapsacks.

Each of them pulled on cords that opened the chutes. The time travelers passed through clouds and looked down on what appeared to them to be an earthly paradise.

"*Que bonita!*" Rosa gasped.

"Fabulous!" Peter cried.

Below them lay a glittering blue lake at least thirty miles long and almost as wide. Towns with beautifully decorated houses and palaces stood on the shores of the lake. There were islands in the lake. One island was a field of flowers, lily ponds, and human-made bathing pools. All points on the lake were connected by causeways and bridges. Canoes plied the waters. Then Peter and Rosa saw a large city of palaces and temples rising from an island in the middle of the lake.

"Those must be the halls of Montezuma!" Peter exclaimed.

"Then that's the city of the Aztecs, just where Quetzie wants us to go," Rosa said.

With a wind blowing behind them, the children pulled at the cords of their chutes and sailed over the lake toward the fabled city of Tenochtitlan.

Gently, easily, they completed their descent and landed at the foot of a grand pyramid. The few steps leading to the plaza on which the pyramid stood seemed to be painted with dark red stripes.

Peter and Rosa wondered if the stripes had been newly painted. They appeared to be dripping. As the travelers climbed the stairs to the plaza, they were overcome by a nasty stench.

"That's not paint!" Rosa was gagging from the smell. "Peter, that's blood! I bet it's human blood!" She pointed. "That slab—it's dripping from looks like an altar!"

Peter found his own voice, gagging. "Human sacrifice! Smoking Mirror must be very much in favor here."

"How awful! He must have become the honcho god in Mexico after he drove Topiltzin away."

"The first thing we have to do is find out what's going on. Look, I see a marketplace just below the end of this plaza."

"I hear voices and I smell food," Rosa said. "Let's check it out."

The children stepped off the plaza by way of a small staircase and entered the marketplace. All manner of fruits and vegetables, such as mangoes, corn, squash, avocados, and beans, were displayed on stone tables. Live turkeys, their feet bound by ropes, hung from obsidian hooks on wooden stalls. Bowls of *posole*, a kind of corn soup, were set on other tables along with chocolate candies and big cigars.

Most of the vendors wore long, white tunics. The men who roamed from booth to booth wore tall feathered headdresses. Peter and Rosa were sure that the men with the tall headdresses were high officials. They were bare-breasted and wore short kilts of various colors that dropped from their waists and fell to their knees. Leather sandals covered their feet, and obsidian daggers hung from their rope belts.

The women wore star-studded blouses, long black skirts, and no shoes. Some wore jade or obsidian necklaces and bracelets. Red cotton shopping bags filled with fruit, vegetables, and other goods were balanced on their heads.

Suddenly, two burly young men confronted Rosa and Peter. They were dressed like the others, except that they wore smoking mirrors over their stomachs.

The young time travelers managed to look away from the mirrors, but the curling smoke caused them to cough. They recognized the mirrors, which were like the ones they had encountered in Tollan I, designed to confuse and humiliate anybody who looked into them. Peter and Rosa stepped back to avoid the smoke. As they did, the two men nodded to one another. Then they fixed their eyes on the children. Both men wore stern expressions on their faces.

"It looks like we are about to become prisoners," Peter said glumly to Rosa.

"We've been prisoners before. Quetzie always sent quetzal birds or something to rescue us," Rosa said.

Peter looked up at the sky. "There isn't a bird in sight. Quetzalcoatl warned us this is the most dangerous mission he's sent us on."

The taller of the two men addressed them in a commanding tone. "Who are you? We've never seen anyone dressed like you before. You are children but—Who sent you here?"

Peter did not understand what the man was saying at first, as he hadn't used the language decoder Quetzalcoatl had implanted in his brain for over two years. He heard buzzing sounds for a few seconds, and finally what it was the Aztecs were saying sounded in his ears like spoken English. He knew then that whatever he said to them would reach their ears in Nahuatl.

But Rosa, who had learned some Nahuatl from her father,

understood everything right away. "We were sent here by Quetzalcoatl," she answered, smiling with pride.

The would-be captors looked at one another in astonishment. Looking back at the children, the tall man spoke again, this time with a nervous tremor in his voice.

"Quetzalcoatl Topiltzin?"

"Topiltzin is the incarnation of Quetzalcoatl, the plumed serpent who sent us here," Rosa said.

"Topiltzin is our friend. He was chased out of Mexico by Smoking Mirror, but he sailed away on a raft with some snakes, vowing to come back some day to claim his throne," Peter explained.

"Claim his throne?" the two men exclaimed in unison. They turned to one another, aghast. "Can it be? Is it true what all the signs seem to be telling us? What will the king say?" the taller man said to his companion. Their faces turned ashen, and they shuddered.

"We must take these children to our lord, Montezuma." They bowed respectfully to Peter and Rosa and gestured for them to accompany them. The children were escorted to the towering pyramid and were told to climb the long staircase. The steps were steep. Both Peter and Rosa were out of breath when they reached the platform on which twin temples stood. There, they saw an old man dressed in a long, white robe. He had a wrinkled face and long dark hair from which long feathers trailed down his back. The old man held a bloodied knife in his hand. When Peter and Rosa approached, they saw two other white-robed men, somewhat younger, wrapping what appeared to be the body of a butchered boy in a sheet and carrying him away. Blood was dripping everywhere. It seemed the boy had been dragged up from the altar below.

"We'll have the gizzards and legs for dinner and give the rest to the pigs," the man with the bloodied knife called after them.

"How horrible!" Rosa exclaimed.

"Will human sacrifice ever end?" Peter said.

Their comments attracted the attention of the man with the bloodied knife. "These children must be from far away," he said, scrutinizing them carefully. "I've never seen such clothes before. Are they to be sacrificed?"

"Your reverence, they come with a message for our great emperor, Lord Montezuma."

His reverence waved his knife in the air and erupted into cackling laugh. "Perhaps when their mission is fulfilled, we can have a feast. Such nice, tender, fresh meat. I will be happy to do the carving." He eyed Rosa and ran his tongue along his lower lip.

The escorts made no reply and led Rosa and Peter over the sparkling white platform to the shadowed area between the two temples. The priest with the knife followed. Sitting on a throne between these twin towers sat the emperor, Montezuma, in all his royal glory. A tall feathered headdress adorned his head. He appeared to be in his midfifties. His face radiated wisdom as well as authority. A jade necklace hung around his neck, from which a pendant, also jade, depicting a cartoon image of a plumed serpent was suspended. The emperor was dressed in a long, light blue cotton robe decorated with bright yellow stars woven into the fabric.

A man who appeared to be another priest stood on one side of the throne holding an open scroll, from which he read. The tall guard approached the emperor, bowed deeply, and whispered something into his ear. The emperor looked at the children in astonishment and smacked his forehead, almost knocking off his feathered headdress.

"Can it be?" he said, looking at the children. He turned to the priests. "Is this another sign? Last night was terrifying enough. I was sleeping in my palace when I awoke to the sound of raging thunder. I ran out on the balcony to see the sky bleeding fire, drop by drop, falling with the rain. Then I saw the temple of our god, Smoking Mirror, struck by lightning. I looked over the edge of the balcony and saw that the sea was boiling. Steaming vapors rose from its bubbly surface. Then I saw a jaguar in the streets, wrapped in the coils of a serpent. Was I dreaming? But no, now these children have come!" He looked directly at Peter and Rosa. "Who are you? Where do you come from? What does your strange clothing represent? What do you want of us?"

He gazed at the children intently as they pondered what answers to give him.

"My guardsman tells me you come on a mission from Quetzalcoatl, but Quetzalcoatl is no more. That is, his human incarnation died a full coil of time ago, lost at sea, never to be seen again. Or—" He checked himself and shook his head. "Or do I speak blasphemy? Do I speak lies? I am told you claim to have known him. Did you know him as Topiltzin, the young king of Tollan II? Tell me then, what does—what did he look like?"

"Oh, he's very handsome," Rosa said.

"And he's a good ballplayer," Peter said. "I played with him."

"Interesting. But I wish to know, what does he look like?"

"Why, he has light skin, like Peter's. And he has a beard. We never saw anyone in these parts with light skin and a beard," Rosa said.

The emperor's eyes opened wide. He turned to the priest with the scroll, who showed him what appeared to be drawings and hieroglyphs. The emperor's mouth fell open, and he smacked his forehead. He was trembling as he faced the children again.

"What were his last words to you?"

"Well," Peter answered, "he was sailing out to sea on a raft of snakes. Just before the raft burst into flames and flew up in the sky, he cried out, 'I will return in one coil of time and reclaim my throne.'"

The emperor rose up, sat down again, and gripped the arms of the throne as if in a desperate effort to prevent it from slipping away from under him. Then he shook his head and shrugged in a gesture of resignation. "Yes, all the signs point to the return of Quetzalcoatl Topiltzin. It is as I prophesied while not wanting to believe my own prophecy." He took a scroll from the priest at his side and scanned it. "Much of my power rests on my ability to read this calendar, which I helped devise. I have studied the stars and read the ancient scriptures. Everything, including your coming today, dear children, tells me that

Topiltzin is about to return to claim his throne, the throne I am sitting on. What he told you when he set out on his raft confirms what I have divined."

The priest unrolled another scroll and pointed out something to the emperor. The emperor struck his forehead again and looked with surprise at the children. He held the scroll up to them.

"Here is a drawing of the two of you standing with Topiltzin just before he set out on his journey."

"Then it is true," said the priest with the bloodied knife, standing on his other side. "But surely, Your Excellency, you cannot let Quetzalcoatl come here. Smoking Mirror is the god who rules our city."

"But by rights, my throne belongs to Quetzalcoatl. It is because of him that I was able to claim the throne in the first place." He turned to the priest holding the scroll. "Remember my coronation? At my inaugural, you told the people I was the descendant of Quetzalcoatl Topiltzin and therefore his natural heir. Of course, it was a lie, but we needed that lie to legitimize my power, and part of me wanted to believe it." He ran his hand over his brow and turned to the children again.

"You see, when our city was founded only two centuries ago, we were the new kids on the block. We conquered our neighbors by brute force. They were older civilizations, rich in learning and tradition. We subdued them over time, and I became emperor thirty years ago. So, in order to gain their respect, we made the claim that I was the heir of Quetzalcoatl Topiltzin. But if he is coming back—and all the signs tell me that he is—I am sure he will demand that I give him back his throne."

The priest with the bloody knife cried out, "No, no, dear king. You must not allow that to happen. We owe all our success to Smoking Mirror. It is thanks to him that we have become the greatest nation there ever was."

Montezuma nodded and then shrugged. "I understand what you are saying. But that is precisely the problem. If Quetzalcoatl comes and demands that I surrender his throne to him, I feel that I must submit to his wish. After all, he is my god. I owe him this throne. But what I fear much more than I fear giving up the throne is that his coming will bring about a war of the gods—a war, I fear, that will cause the destruction of the world as we know it. I must do everything in my power to prevent Quetzalcoatl Topiltzin from coming."

The priests smiled and dropped to their knees before Montezuma, kissing his cloak. The priest with the scroll spoke. "O wisest of all monarchs, most excellent of excellencies, we pledge our loyalty and service to you. But what do you propose to do that will keep the great serpent god at bay?"

The emperor leaned forward, running his finger along his chin, deep in thought. Then he straightened up and lifted his finger in the air. "I know." He snapped his fingers. "There is a treasury hidden in my father's old palace. It contains all the wealth my father amassed in his long life. If I receive word that Topiltzin is on his way here, I will send ambassadors bearing heaping bags of gold, silver, and jade to meet him on his way and present the treasures to him as gifts from me. Then they will explain to him, with all due respect, that I advise him to accept the gifts for the sake of peace in both heaven and earth and then return to that place from whence he came."

The priests looked at one another with down-turned lips and shrugged. It was obvious that they were not convinced by what Montezuma had said. Montezuma shrugged and looked about as if he had not convinced himself that his strategy would work. "Topiltzin will heed my advice, won't he? I mean, he will accept my offering of gold and go back to where he came from. He must, I tell you. What do you think?"

The priests responded with a little throat clearing but did not speak. They then fixed their eyes on Peter and Rosa. "And what of these children?" the priest with the scroll said. "They claim to be sent by Quetzalcoatl."

"I say fresh meat," the priest with the bloodied knife said. "I think the little girl would make a nice, tender steak."

Rosa responded with fury. "Don't you dare! What you do think Quetzalcoatl would do to you if you even touched one of us?"

The priest laughed, but Montezuma silenced him. "It would be a terrible mistake to harm these children. I have reason to believe their story. If we harm them in any way, Quetzalcoatl will surely wreak havoc upon us. That alone could lead to a war of the gods. Not only Quetzalcoatl and Smoking Mirror but Tlaloc, the rain god, and Huitzapitl, the god of the sun, will become involved. Our world will be torn apart. It will surely be the end of the Fifth Sun and, most likely, of all humanity." Montezuma was on the verge of tears.

"How did Smoking Mirror become so special here?" Rosa asked.

"We needed him. After all, he is the god of war. When we came here, we were surrounded by enemies. We needed Smoking Mirror on our side. He gave us the courage and strength to conquer our enemies. In return, he demanded human sacrifice. We had to pay Smoking Mirror and other gods with human blood. We gave them the blood of many of the finest people we conquered. In order to maintain our power, we must still pay him with human sacrifice."

"That's awful!" Rosa said. "I hope that when Quetzalcoatl Topiltzin comes, he will end human sacrifice the way he did in Tollan."

Montezuma shook his head and smiled sadly. "Oh, that it could be so," he said to them. "Now, since you were sent here by the god in whose name I rule this empire, I will take you to a room in my palace reserved for special guests."

"Thank you, Your Excellency," Rosa and then Peter said.

Two servants appeared to lead the children down the steps of the Templo Mayor and to the palace. Peter and Rosa realized that Tenochtitlan was a city built around canals. The houses they passed seemed to be made of hard, orange-brown clay.

Then they entered a grand palace and walked through a courtyard built around a lovely pool where water lilies floated, gold fish swam between them, and turtles sunned on rocks.

The children were led to a large room with two good-sized beds covered with feathered mattresses and cotton blankets. After they settled in, the servants reappeared to take them to a huge dining room where Montezuma and some priests and lords sat at a long table. They all enjoyed a dinner of enchiladas with baked crabs, rice and beans, and steaming chocolate. "This is the kind of food my aunt in the USA serves," Rosa said to Peter.

"I can't wait to visit her when we get back," Peter said.

Then, having had a very eventful day, the children returned to their room. They fell asleep as soon as their heads touched the feathered pillows.

Chapter 5

In the morning, the children were ushered into the dining room where Montezuma sat alone. He did not look happy and greeted the children with a forced smile. The children were each presented with a dish of eggs swimming in a spicy tomato sauce, refried beans, tortillas, cups of mango juice, and steaming chocolate. They devoured their breakfast with gusto. Montezuma ate little and said little.

"You look very worried," Rosa said to him at last.

The emperor shrugged and offered a weary smile. "Yes. I am very concerned for our future—not only mine but that of the world as I have come to know it."

Suddenly, some bustling sounds came from the plaza outside the palace. Excited voices were heard followed by the sound of sandaled feet slapping against tiles. Montezuma rose from his throne as a young warrior dressed only in a loin cloth wrapped around his waist and sandals entered the room. He was accompanied by two palace guards. The visitor was out of breath and sweating. He held a scroll in his hands.

"Well, what's the news? Has he come—the god I am expecting?" the emperor asked impatiently.

The warrior could not speak at first but nodded his head. "Yes," he finally managed to say. "I am the last of ten relay runners who set out from Tabasco, and I come with a message sent by your ambassador there."

"And how did he arrive—Quetzalcoatl Topiltzin, I mean? Did he come as he set out a coil of time ago, on a raft accompanied by snakes? On a canoe?"

"The story is told in this scroll." The warrior handed the scroll to the emperor.

The emperor began to unroll the parchment and then shook his head in frustration. "Ah, the print is much too small for me. My eyes have gone bad. Guard!" he called out. "Summon Priest Scribe of Scrolls at once. I want him to read this message aloud."

The guard left the room swiftly and returned almost immediately with the priest who had shown the emperor the scroll that contained the drawings of Peter and Rosa the day before. As he began to unroll the scroll sent from Tabasco, the children could see that the print was much smaller than in the other scrolls.

"Your Excellency," the scribe began, "it is written here that the person answering to your description of Quetzalcoatl Topiltzin arrived in our vassal city, Tabasco, three days ago. If he is, indeed, the lord god you are awaiting, his arrival comes just as he promised a coil of time ago and just as you have predicted."

Montezuma nodded vigorously. He was very excited now. "Go on, go on. How did he arrive? By sea? Did he come in a canoe? A raft? Did he drop down from the sky?"

"Very interesting," the scribe read on. "He and his troop of guardsmen arrived in three giant vessels of a sort never seen by our kind. They seemed to be propelled by the wind blowing against massive cotton drapes hanging from tall masts."

Montezuma slapped his cheek. "Of course! Among his other powers, Quetzalcoatl—the heavenly Quetzalcoatl, that is—is the god of wind. It was he who took a deep breath and created the wind that lifted the fifth sun from the sea, giving birth to our world. But did they come ashore, Topiltzin and his men? Did our Tabascans attack them?"

"At first, the Tabascans gathered their forces to attack," the scribe read on. "After all, there are thousands of Tabascans, their fighters all well-armed. The invaders consisted of no more than five hundred men. But by the time our loyal Tabascans were ready to attack, a strange thing happened. Many of the invaders set sail for our shore in small canoes. As they drew near, the Tabascans were astonished to see some very strange creatures among them, creatures they could not have believed existed. These creatures appeared to be half human and half beast. Their upper parts—head, arms, and torso—were human, though dressed in clothes we've never seen. Their lower parts, everything from the waist down, seemed to be those of giant, fur-coated animal. Some were brown; some were black. They were much larger than jaguars, having four legs and, strangest of all, long necks and a long head in addition to their human heads."

"By all the gods! What did you all do?" Montezuma gasped.

"Just as our Tabascan forces were about to send spears and arrows against them, loud thunder broke out from the giant canoes. Huge balls made of something hard as volcanic rock came at us faster than bolts of lightning. They didn't strike anyone. Rather, they seemed to be sent as a warning. That's what Chief of the Spears believed, and he ordered his warriors to hold back.

"'Surely it is as our lord Montezuma foretold,'" Priest Scribe of Scrolls read on. "'We are witnessing the arrival of the god Quetzalcoatl Topiltzin, the incarnation of the plumed serpent.' Just then the god himself, wearing a helmet shining like silver and some kind of metal armor, stepped out of the lead canoe. He wore tall leather boots as he waded to shore. All the Tabascans fell to their knees before him. Chief Lord of Spears kissed the earth and then the feet of his reverence."

"And what did he look like?" Montezuma asked eagerly.

"It says here that he was very majestic looking, very commanding—yes, godlike. He was handsome, a young man in his midthirties, pale-faced with a dark beard that grew down his chin."

Montezuma ran his hand along his own beardless chin. "Pale faced?

A beard. Only one person in all our history had a pale face and beard. That was Topiltzin! Do we need further proof?" He leaned forward now in the direction of the scribe. "Does the scroll say anything about the gifts of gold and silver I sent?"

"I don't see—" the scribe turned the scroll over. "Here, there's something on the other side. Yes, it reads here that the godlike visitor was very pleased with the gifts you sent and sends gifts in return."

The messenger slid off a knapsack that had been strapped to his back and pulled out handfuls of shiny bracelets and necklaces.

Montezuma looked at the trinkets in awe. "These gems could only have been made from material that exists in heaven," he marveled, fondling them.

"They are made from cheap glass," Rosa whispered to Peter with a small giggle.

"I will place them in the temple of the sun god," Montezuma said. He turned to the scribe again. "Did Chief Lord of Spears thank him for his visit and wish him a fine journey home?"

"Yes, he did, just as you requested through your ambassador."

"And how did Topiltzin respond?"

The scribe hesitated before reading on. "Your Excellency, it says here that the god, if god he be, spoke through a translator. Presumably, his native language is not the same as ours."

Montezuma nodded. "Yes, of course. The language Topiltzin spoke was Toltec, the language of the inhabitants of Tollan, a coil of time ago. But who was the translator?"

"Let me see. Here it is. Her name was Malinche, a beautiful young woman and one of our own, a Mexican with smooth reddish skin and long, dark hair, dressed in a pale-blue gown and wearing a jade necklace. She was living with a Tabascan family, as her parents had died when she was a little girl, but she had lived in Cuba, an island off the coast that was settled by sailors from beyond the rising sun twenty years ago. It is from them that she learned the language spoken by the god."

"Fascinating." Montezuma stroked his chin. "So Topiltzin comes to visit us from a land beyond the sunrise. But come, how did Topiltzin respond to my thanking him for his visit and wishing him a fine journey home?"

The scribe sighed deeply before going on. "Yes, he thanks you for your good wishes but says he is coming here to see you."

On hearing this, Montezuma uttered a woeful cry. "No, no, he mustn't come. Couldn't Chief Lord of Spears discourage him? Why didn't he explain the problems with the trip—steep mountains, treacherous rivers, violent bandits? After all, he may be a god, but he is incarnated in human form."

Priest Scribe of Scrolls shrugged. "Yes, apparently all those things were pointed out to him, but he insisted on coming."

The emperor clenched his fists and shook his head. "No! No! No! We must send messengers to give Topiltzin fresh gifts and urge him to return to heaven or wherever he came from. Dispatch fresh messengers at once. I await their return."

When the messenger set out on his mission, Montezuma turned to the children. "I am going to my bedroom to practice dream divination. I need the guidance that dreams may bring. You may want to go outside to get some fresh air. I will send guards who will take you to a gondolier who will give you a canoe ride in the canal."

"A canoe ride? That sounds lovely," Rosa said.

"It sure does," Peter agreed.

The two guards who had first greeted Rosa and Peter appeared to escort them along the canal that ran just below the palace. They didn't have to walk long before they saw a canoe docked along the wide canal. The guards spoke to the gondolier, and the children boarded.

It was a lovely ride. They went out on the lake, passed some small islands, and beheld the cities that lined the shore all around.

"There must be hundreds of thousands of people living here if you count all those living around the lake," Peter said.

"I had no idea the capital of the Aztecs could be so big," Rosa said. "My father never told me. He said it was a terrible time in our history and I was too young to hear about it. I was only six when my parents brought me to your country."

"*Our* country, Rosa," Peter corrected her gently. 'You've lived in it eight years. That's more than half your life. It's your country now as well as mine."

Rosa nodded her head and smiled. "I guess you're right, Peter. I'm an American, no matter how you look at it."

Yes, she had changed in many ways, Peter thought to himself. Not only was she less quarrelsome, at least with him, but she was becoming a real beauty. Then he reminded himself, *You are both facing serious problems, the most serious you've ever had. And you have no way to contact Quetzalcoatl. You've got to think hard, find a way to face the catastrophe brewing all around you.*

"Getting back to where we are now and what we have to face," he said, "if this is such a terrible time for Mexico as your father said, we're really in for it. And Montezuma has every right to be worried. Do you really think it was Topiltzin who landed in Tabasco with three big windjammers and a small army? Or was it the Spaniards? I haven't studied world history in school yet."

Rosa knitted her brow. "I know the Spaniards invaded Mexico, but I don't know when or what happened."

"I think we're about to find out. The name Montezuma is familiar to me. There's a song that goes, 'From the halls of Montezuma to the shores of Tripoli.' I don't know where Tripoli is, but I'm sure the halls of Montezuma are in Mexico and our private room is in one of them."

"Well," Rosa said with a little laugh, "Topiltzin or Spanish explorer—maybe they are the same. Maybe Topiltzin went to Spain when he left Tollan and came back with a Spanish army."

Peter erupted into laughter. "Rosa, you come up with some of the wackiest ideas!"

Rosa had been running her hand along the water in the lake, and as Peter continued to laugh, she pulled her hand out and splashed water in Peter's face. "Chill out, *Gringo Tonto*," she teased him.

Peter, still laughing, thrust an arm over his side of the canoe, came up with a big handful of water mixed with seaweed, and threw it with force at Rosa.

He threw it harder than he intended, and she was dazed. Some of it went into her eyes, and she couldn't see.

"I'm sorry, Rosa, really." He pulled a clean handkerchief out of his pocket and carefully wiped her face. As he ran the cloth over her cheeks, he experienced a thrill more intense than he had ever felt before. He ran the handkerchief around her ears and along her neck. Neither of them spoke but gazed, speechless, into one another's eyes. The gondolier laughed and began to sing as he continued to dip his oar into the lake.

Chapter 6

When the youngsters returned to the palace, they saw that a council was being held in the main courtyard. Sitting with Montezuma were several high priests and military commanders, the highest ranking being General Heart on Fire. He was studying a map given him by Priest Scribe of Scrolls. "This is where the enemy will arrive," the general said, pointing to the village across the lake where the main bridge to Tenochtitlan began. "Topiltzin and his army will descend into the valley from the surrounding mountains. All our spies tell us they are cutting a wide swath, visiting all our vassal states to recruit rebels who will join their fight against us. There is no question that his aim is to destroy our empire. We must do to Topiltzin what Smoking Mirror did to him in the last coil of time. Only we must do more than banish him. We must kill him, once and for all."

There were many shouts of "Hear! Hear! Let's do it!" from the assembled company of military officers and priests. Only a few, such as Priest Scribe of Scrolls, wanted to meet Topiltzin in peace. "There is no real evidence that Topiltzin wants war with us," he said.

"Your Excellency," Chief Heart on Fire continued, "you are our emperor. It is to you that the gods have given authority over our empire. You sit on the throne of Quetzalcoatl Topiltzin, but it is Smoking Mirror we have to thank for the great empire that is ours. We call on you to lead us in the struggle against Topiltzin. Tell us, O holy one—give us the order to bring death to Quetzalcoatl Topiltzin and defeat his army."

Montezuma looked on in distress as the group began to shout, "What do we want? War! War now! War now!"

The great emperor ran his hands over his ears and looked at his compatriots in despair. "You make a strong case," he said to Chief Heart on Fire, "and most of our high officials agree with you. But give me time. I must pray for divine guidance."

"We have little time to spare," Chief Heart on Fire said.

"I will give you my decision when I can," Montezuma said.

With that, the meeting broke up. The officials left, leaving Montezuma with Priest Scribe of Scrolls and Peter and Rosa. He buried his head in his hands.

"I just don't know," he muttered, half to himself. He lifted his tearstained face. "It seems there is one course of action. Chief Heart on Fire has put it clearly. He has won wide support among the lords and military staff, and I'm sure he's winning over the people. Yet in my heart, I am not convinced."

"Can't you see?" Peter said. "Chief Heart on Fire and those who support him want to get rid of *you*. If you kill Topiltzin, you will be giving up your right to the throne. Without that right, you cannot call yourself emperor, and the people will not support you."

"And maybe Topiltzin doesn't really want to sit on your throne," Rosa said. "He sent you gifts and thanked you for the gifts you sent him. When we knew him back in Tollan II, he was against war and did all he could to avoid it."

Montezuma looked at Peter and Rosa with a kindly smile. "Yes," he said. "You are wise children. I'm beginning to understand why Quetzalcoatl sent you to me."

"That may very well be our mission," Rosa said.

Chapter 7

⁓

The next day, another messenger, dressed in loin cloth and sandals, came running through the halls of Montezuma. When he entered the throne room, he dropped to his knees and bowed his head before the emperor. The children were sitting with him.

"Do you come with news from our visitor from far away?" Montezuma asked, cutting through all formalities and waiting anxiously for the messenger to catch his breath.

"Yes," he said at last. "He has departed Tlaxcala and is on his way here."

"Tlaxcala?" Montezuma was surprised. "He is taking a long, roundabout route. As he landed in Vera Cruz, which is on the sea and to the north of here, why did he go to Tlaxcala? Tlaxcala is in the Sierra Mountains and north of here. This does not bode well."

Montezuma rose from his throne and shook his fists in the air. "Tlaxcala is the rebel state completely out of our control! It has defied us throughout our reign. The Tlaxcalans pay us no tribute of any kind, no victims for human sacrifice! They have threatened to take other vassal states away from us. And they have a large military force. Did they offer our visitor any troops?"

The messenger shook his head and opened empty hands. "They offered him ten thousand soldiers. You know they have the largest army in Mexico next to ours."

"Ten thousand troops?" The emperor gripped his cheeks in his hands. "Gods help us. I am now convinced that the cosmic war will soon begin. The world as we know it will be destroyed." The emperor wept openly.

Rosa rushed to comfort the grieving Montezuma. "Don't cry." She stroked his shoulder. "It can't be all that bad. Remember, Quetzalcoatl is the god of life and peace. I think he only wants to restore the harmony among the gods that has been lost with so much fighting and human sacrifice."

"I can only hope you are right," Montezuma sobbed, kissing her hand. "I was never in favor of human sacrifice, not on the scale we practiced it. But if Topiltzin comes with a huge army of Tlaxcalans as well as Tabascans, there will be a war on a scale the world has never seen."

Peter and Rosa only nodded and hung their heads.

Chapter 8

~~~

That night, the children were awakened by a great rumble that shook them in their beds. They got up and ran out to the terrace that overlooked the cities and distant mountains. Montezuma, dressed in his stocking nightcap and blue evening gown, stood at the end of the terrace, gripping the wooden railing. Far in the distance, they all saw a giant spear of fire rising from the mouth of a great, snow-covered volcano. The flame rose straight up as a pillar, reaching to the stars, and appeared to brush the underside of Venus, the morning star.

"Surely, it is another sign," the emperor said. "The god is marching with all his forces between the great volcanoes Popocatepetl and Istacciuatl. Popocatepetl, the great warrior of the legend, stands watch over the sleeping princess, Istacciuatl. Now he holds his torch aloft to greet the god Topiltzin and light his way over the pass between the two volcanoes."

Neither Montezuma nor the time travelers went back to their rooms to sleep but stayed awake, watching the sky until dawn. As the sun rose, Montezuma, who had said nothing since his remarks about the spear of flame, came to a decision. "The only hope is more gold, buckets of it. It is my understanding from our last messenger that the man-god prefers gold to any gift I can offer him. I will send five scouts to meet Topiltzin and his army when they arrive at the bottom of the pass between the mighty peaks. If enough gold is offered him, it is my fervent wish he will honor my request and turn homeward across the sea, or wherever his home may be. I will have the emissaries direct him to gold mines he may help himself to on his way back to the sea."

Within an hour, the gifts were assembled, and the emissaries, accompanied by a dozen warriors, set out. Montezuma and the children watched them cross the causeway that spanned the lake.

Montezuma spent the next few days pacing up and down the palace floors, tugging at his graying locks and muttering to himself. Peter and Rosa became edgy watching him. On the third day, two scouts appeared, sweating profusely but smiling broadly. Montezuma ran to them. "Tell me, what's the news?"

"Good news, Your Excellency. Quetzalcoatl Topiltzin, if he be so named, is now resting on the southern shore of the lake and is only a day's journey from here."

"Wonderful, but did he accept the gold? Did he promise to leave?"

"He accepted the gold and wants to thank you personally. He says it is important that he visit you before he leaves."

Montezuma shook his head and frowned. "Then I am doomed," he said bitterly. "How large is his military force? Did he bring a large army of Tlaxcalans and other former vassals? Do they come bearing spears, obsidian swords, hatchets? If so, I will not be able to keep the lords of Smoking Mirror from striking back with all their might."

The scouts laughed and waved their hands in the air. "Your majesty, there is no army of Tlaxcalans. The god comes with only a few hundred of his own men and a small band of Tabascans. They have some strange weapons that shoot out hard black balls and some strange creatures they ride on called horses. But the god says he comes in peace and friendship."

Montezuma's face lit up. "Peace and friendship," he repeated softly, savoring the words.

"And he comes with a very small military force. That alone should hold the lords of Smoking Mirror in check. As for me, I will set out to greet him." The emperor smiled and rubbed his hands in glee. "Servants!" he called out. A dozen servants came at once as if from out of cracks in the walls. "Prepare my litter! Bring me my robe and staff of gold!"

Six servants ran outside while the others ran back to the inner rooms, returning with a bright blue robe decorated with yellow stars. "Prepare my father's palace to lodge our guests," he said as a servant draped the jade medal around his neck.

Montezuma then turned to Peter and Rosa. "I want you to go to the palace where Topiltzin will be received. You will tell me if you recognize him. That will be the final test, eh?"

"We knew him five hundred years ago. I'm sure he's changed, taken on a different form since then," Peter said.

"Have *you* changed?" Montezuma asked.

"Well, not so much. We are both two years older."

"Plus a few thousand years, one way or another," Rosa said, laughing.

"Well, I wish you a happy reunion." Montezuma chuckled.

With that, they all went outside where the royal litter waited. The roof of the litter was covered with shiny green and blue quetzal feathers. The doors and windows of the carriage were lined with silver and gold. The emperor climbed aboard, and six runners, three on either side of the carriage, lifted it from the ground and set out on the causeway to Tacuba.

As the young visitors and servants watched, Rosa said to Peter, "You know, I just realized that Montezuma looks a lot like my father as I remember him. He carries himself with the same dignity and style. And he's very kind at heart."

Chapter 9

~~

Peter and Rosa were awed by the splendor of the palace that had been the home of Montezuma's father, Face of Waters. They were ushered into a large, open courtyard. In the center, a fountain sent up a stream of water twenty feet high. It rose from a pool in which goldfish swam among blossoming water lilies. Frogs sunned themselves on rocks. There were many rooms around the courtyard with cotton drapes hanging on walls. Many bore murals, one of which showed Topiltzin flying up in the sky with his raft of snakes on fire.

As they continued their exploration of the palace, the children were horrified to see the old priest whom they had seen when they first climbed the pyramid of the twin towers. They recognized the long nose and chin that gave his head the shape of an axe, the deep-set eyes that seemed to demand the attention of everyone they focused on. The old priest cackled merrily upon seeing the children. He held his blood-encrusted knife in one hand. In the middle of the room lay a stone block that dripped with red streaks and gave forth the stench of blood. The stench caused Peter and Rosa to cough and back away.

"Ah, at last," the old priest said with a laugh that rebounded from the walls. "How wonderful! Fate has brought you to me. What a delightful surprise! All signs tell me you have been sent to me so that I may prepare you for the royal feast that will be held when the emperor returns with his guests. Yes, you will provide delicious food for his majesty's table. He will not need to know where such tender meat came from. He can be sentimental about such things, and we must condone his tendency to feel pity. Ah, little girl, you are ideally suited to become the main dish. Such lovely arms, legs—and I adore those tiny feet. What fine morsels they will make. Yummy, yummy, yum. Come to me, my sweet meat." He beckoned with the middle finger of his free hand.

"Don't you dare," Rosa cried. "We were not sent here to be sacrificed for anybody's dinner. If Montezuma knew you had such thoughts, he would sacrifice *you*."

"Oh, how you talk! Here's my answer." He turned toward the entrance of the next room and called out, "Palace guards!"

Two muscular young men wearing loin cloths wrapped around their waists and bearing swords trimmed with glassy volcanic rock appeared.

"Help the young lady to rest comfortably on the altar," the priest said while scraping his blood-encrusted knife against a sharpened stone.

As the guards advanced, Peter threw himself between them and Rosa. "Don't you dare touch her!" he shouted. One of the guards lashed at him with his sword. Peter stepped aside with lightning speed and caught the guard's hand as it came down with the sword. In one swift movement, he twisted the sword free of the guard's hand. Using the sword, Peter beat the guard who went howling out of the room. He out-dueled the second guard, knocking his dark, glassy sword out of his hand. Suddenly, two new guards appeared wielding stone hatchets. Peter tried to fight them off, but in the scuffle, the guard who had run off returned with a new sword. Peter was surrounded now. Attacked from all sides, he fell to the floor.

Rosa was seized and stretched on her back over the altar. The old priest laughed joyously and approached the altar with his bloody knife poised to strike. Peter struggled to get up but was beaten down again, his head bleeding from the cuts he had received.

Just then, a stranger wearing a sparkling iron helmet and a vest woven from strands of dark metal appeared. He was light-skinned and had a pointed beard. The stranger carried a metal sword in one hand and a pistol in the other. Driving two of the guardsmen away with his sword, he fired his pistol so that it splintered the obsidian sword held by another. He fired another shot that knocked a hatchet out of a guard's hand. Now all the guards threw up their hands and huddled against the wall.

The old priest shuddered with fright as the stranger loosened the bonds that strapped Rosa to the altar. Once freed, Rosa sat up in disbelief. She and Peter looked at their rescuer in wonder. As they did, he fixed his eyes on the priest. "There shall be no more human sacrifice," he said. His voice was like thunder. "Those are my orders and the orders of my father in heaven. You will obey them if you place any value on your lives."

"Your Excellency," the old priest said, his voice shaking as he attempted to justify his actions, "our empire was founded on the practice of human sacrifice. If we end it—"

"Not another word, old crow, or with my pistol, I will do to your head what I did to your servant's sword. Now be off, all of you. Out of my sight!"

Although the children's language decoder enabled them to hear what was being said in English, they were sure the priest did not understand what the foreigner was saying. Yet his voice was so commanding, it was enough to drive the Aztec natives away.

When they left, the ironclad stranger looked at the children and smiled. He was young, appearing in his midthirties. He was handsome and, although he did resemble Topiltzin as they had known him, having a beard, light skin, and all, he was shorter. Yet he had that aura of godlike authority about him.

"Thank you very much for saving our lives," Rosa said, wiping away tears from her eyes.

"My pleasure," their savior said, smiling. "It's just that I abhor human sacrifice. I will see that it is ended here once and for all!"

"Then you must be—" Peter began to say but decided to check himself. "That is, you seemed to know already what the old priest was trying to tell you about the history of human sacrifice in these parts."

The savior's eyes widened, and he smiled. "I can see that you are very smart young people. You must be strangers yourselves. Your clothing is nothing like the clothing I've seen the natives wear. I'm sure you are from a faraway place."

"Yes, we are," Rosa said, "but if I may say so, your own clothing suggests that you too are from a faraway place."

Their new friend and savior smiled again. "Yes, I am from a place far across the sea. But from everything I gathered as I was escorted across the lake, although you may be from a faraway place, you are friends of Montezuma. Am I right?"

"Yes," Rosa replied. "We are very lucky to have been guests in his palace. We had an introduction, so to speak. We have found Montezuma to be a very nice man. We can tell you that in his heart, he is opposed to human sacrifice. But all the priests and the lords of Smoking Mirror insist on it. The emperor has trouble dealing with them on that point, as it could lead to a civil war. However, we are sure that Montezuma will be your friend."

"Good. Bernal, one of my officers, tells me he has been very kind to my men. He has showered them with gifts of gold and jewels. And he has given me a most royal welcome. He has housed me in this beautiful palace. However, I don't like the neighborhood. There is a zoo next door. The animals are fed the hearts and other bodily parts of humans who have been sacrificed. I tried to tell His Excellency, the emperor, that his religion is one in which the gods are devils. He only scoffs and tells me that his religion works. One proof is that following the signs given him by his gods, he was able to predict my coming almost to the very day! But I am puzzled as to why Montezuma has been so nice to me. To be sure, I have come with a small army so that he will know I do not want to bring a war. But what does Montezuma think of me? Did he tell you? I need your help. I must decide what I should do."

"He sees you as divine," Peter said, "but he hopes you will accept his hospitality as well as the gifts he will bestow upon you and go away in peace."

"You must know," Rosa put in, "that, above all, Montezuma wants to avoid a war of the gods. Such a war could bring about the destruction of the world. For Montezuma, saving the world for all of humanity is more important than his continuing to be emperor of Mexico."

The great warrior's jaw dropped. He broke into a wide smile. "Of course! You have revealed something very important to me. Thanks to you, I am given a great insight. I now know how I should go about achieving my goal, which was set for me by my own god. Yes, I will tell Montezuma that I intend to help him accomplish his mission of saving the world!"

He pulled the youngsters to his breast and hugged them. "What wise and lovely young people you are. Absolute angels. I am to meet with Montezuma in his palace tomorrow. I would like you to come with me. Yes, thanks to you, my sights are set. I will call servants to escort you to your room. Don't worry—they won't be carrying bloody knives." They all laughed together. "*Hasta mañana,*" the godlike commander said.

When he left, the children looked at one another in astonishment. "Did you hear that?" Peter asked Rosa.

"Yes, he said *hasta mañana*. That's Spanish for *see you tomorrow*." Peter shrugged.

"It must have been a slip in our wiring. Maybe Topiltzin did go to Spain when he descended from heaven, and that's where he gathered an army to win back Montezuma's throne."

"You could be right, Rosa, but is it Montezuma's throne he wants? I wish I knew my history better. Something tells me that Spain conquered Mexico. I don't know when."

Rosa wrinkled her brow, a sign that she was thinking hard. "Maybe that's what my father was hinting at. He knew Nahuatl, the language Montezuma speaks. Of course, my pop spoke Spanish in his everyday life. I was brought up speaking Spanish. What year was it that the Spanish came here?"

Peter tapped his chin with a finger. "Let me see. We knew Topiltzin in the year one thousand. When he left, he said he would return to claim his throne in a coil of time. That's five hundred years."

"Of course!" Rosa exclaimed excitedly. "Now I remember. 1519! That's the year the Spaniards invaded Mexico."

Peter knitted his brow and shook a fist. "Yes. What was that song again? The halls of Montezuma. We may be very well be living in the year 1519 now. So what are we doing here? Why did Quetzalcoatl send us? What does he want from us?"

Rosa shrugged and raised her eyes. "Stay tuned," she said.

The children laughed together. As they did, Rosa ran a hand over one of Peter's shoulders. Peter was thrilled.

Chapter 10

⟨~⟩

The next morning, the man believed to be the second coming of Topiltzin, his officers, Peter and Rosa, and Malinche, the translator, now known as Doña Marina, set out to meet Montezuma. They were admitted into the royal palace and escorted by servants into Montezuma's presence. The emperor rose from his throne and knelt before his distinguished visitor, bowing and kissing his feet. "Welcome, O divine one," Montezuma repeated several times. "I hope you are pleased with the palace I have reserved for you. I do my best to worship you as you deserve."

The commander stood erect, his arms folded over his chest. "The palace is fine. But I did not come here for you to worship me. I want you to grant me the power that is due me."

Montezuma's face fell. His worst imaginings were coming true. Quetzalcoatl Topiltzin was demanding his throne. "Yes, of course," he forced himself to say. "After all, it has been prophesied that you would come to claim the throne that I have been sitting on throughout my reign as emperor." He hung his head. "I must submit. I only hope my lords and priests will not stand in the way."

His advisors, standing with him, nodded in silent agreement, although many of them grumbled.

"It is not so bad for you as you may think," his awesome visitor said. "I have plans to expand your powers. But in order for us to clear up the question of what will be your authority and what will be mine, I must ask you to move over to Lord Face of Water's palace with me. There we will discuss what your rule will consist of in the future and what will be mine."

After absorbing Doña Marina's translation, Montezuma gasped. His advisors appeared stunned. "You want me to be your prisoner in the house of my father?"

"My prisoner? You mustn't look at it that way. You may bring your family with you, your whole court, if you wish, and I insist you bring these delightful children. You will be at liberty to come and go as you please. In the end, you will become a better ruler than you are today."

Rosa and Peter looked at one another in astonishment. "But you are asking me to leave my palace," Montezuma said. "That is an offense. You are denying me my powers as emperor of this nation." Montezuma scowled. "The lords of Smoking Mirror will not accept that. They are displeased with your being here as it is. I fear a rebellion. And what will my people say, those who see me as a messenger of the divine?"

"And who is that divinity? From whence do you derive your powers? You must tell your people that you are doing what the gods have commanded."

Trembling, his face a sickly white, Montezuma bowed deeply. "And you are the god who commands me."

Chapter 11

~

In the beginning, Montezuma adapted well to his confinement in Lord Face of Water's palace. He was able to continue his rule. His lords were permitted to visit him and carry out his orders for governing Tenochtitlan and the cities around the lake. He was even permitted to preside over a ceremony honoring the gods while he sat on his throne between the twin towers.

He came to accept Topiltzin II (as he was called) as his spiritual master. It could be said that they became friends. They dined together, enjoying well-prepared servings of duck, turkey, oysters swimming in chocolate sauce, and mango juice, all served by Doña Marina, who also acted as translator. Peter and Rosa took their meals with them and were treated with affection by both Montezuma and the presumed Topiltzin. One afternoon after lunch, Topiltzin II, after having taken a measure of Montezuma's interest in board games, recommended a game. Looking on, Peter and Rosa were reminded of the game of chess. As both players had experience in governing and planning, they each showed great skill in deciding what moves to make and how to outguess one another. In the end, Topiltzin II won, finally claiming Montezuma's king.

"You've won, fair and square." Montezuma smiled with a wave of his hand.

"Yes. I have claimed your king. But this is just a game. I ask you to take it as a sign of what I want from you in the real world."

"A sign?" Montezuma drew himself up. "You speak in such riddles, your holiness. What can you want from me that I haven't given you already? You have control over my throne, my authority, all my buckets of gold."

Topiltzin shook his head. "There is something more I want you to do for me. I serve another emperor who lives far across the sea. I must ask you to sign away your claim to the throne of Mexico to him."

Montezuma was horror-struck. All color faded from his cheeks. It would have been better if Topiltzin II had struck him with his sword. "An emperor other than me? I accept you as my master. You are the god I owe allegiance to. How can you expect me to give up my throne to one who is only human? My lords will not accept it."

Topiltzin II did not reply right away. It was as if he did not know how to answer. "You must understand," he said at last. "My mission is to bring this land and all its people under the authority of the great God of creation." Topiltzin nodded to Doña Marina, who produced a paper which she placed before the emperor. "It is essential that you sign this paper giving all your authority to my master, Charles V. He is the emperor of the land across the sea."

Montezuma felt his heart beating hard against his chest. His mind whirled about in confusion. "How can he be your master?" he protested. "He is only a human, like me, and you are a god."

Topiltzin paused again, his brow wrinkling as he struggled to make his case convincing. "This is true, but Charles V has dedicated his life to serving that very God of creation. Surely, you believe in such a god."

Montezuma struggled to collect his thoughts. "Yes, I believe in a God of creation. He created the world as well as all the gods who serve him. But he is busy with matters concerning far away stars, galaxies. Other gods, such as Quetzalcoatl, who is your father, and Smoking Mirror are responsible for the world. So it is decreed. I am absolutely sure my lords and my people will not accept my giving away my crown to an emperor across the sea." Montezuma shook his head in a firm resolve.

"But it is necessary," Topiltzin responded. "My authority to guide you must come from the emperor who serves the God of creation. Otherwise I have no authority at all. And as I am the god who gave you your throne, you must obey me."

Montezuma threw up his hands in despair.

Peter and Rosa looked at one another in wonder.

"Do you really believe that man who is giving orders to Montezuma is really the second coming of Topiltzin?" Rosa whispered to Peter.

"It all fits in with the prophecies Montezuma has made," Peter answered, "and that man saved our lives."

"Yes, that's what Topiltzin would do. I just feel something strange is going on here," Rosa said.

Just then, two of Montezuma's priests entered the room. Montezuma took them aside. Peter and Rosa heard Montezuma explain the demands that were being made on him. The priests shook their heads in outrage. "We fear that bad things will come of this, Lord Montezuma. But if you insist."

"I must insist," Montezuma said gloomily.

The ceremony was held the next day on the platform between the twin towers. Doña Marina acted as the secretary who drew up the papers in two languages. The Mexicans in attendance wept. Montezuma wept as he signed the papers. Some of the soldiers otherwise loyal to Topiltzin II wept openly, as they had become fond of Montezuma. Peter and Rosa looked on with a mixture of sadness and hope that, though a war might be inevitable, it would not be as catastrophic as Montezuma feared.

Chapter 12

❧

Many lords and priests were unhappy that Montezuma had signed away his and their rights to some faraway emperor.

"It may be true that the invader is indeed Quetzalcoatl Topiltzin," Lord Maize Cob said to Montezuma after the presumed god left the ceremony to attend to other business, "but remember it was Smoking Mirror who drove Topiltzin out of Mexico a coil of time ago, and it is Smoking Mirror who must drive him out again."

"I have done everything I can to avoid a war of the gods. I fear the end of our world."

"You have signed away our world," Lord Maize Cob said.

Montezuma slumped and shook his head in despair.

"It may be out of our hands," Lord Hatchet Face said. "Our people are becoming restless. I fear a revolt. You are our emperor. But we cannot guarantee that we can stem a revolution."

When the lords left, Montezuma turned to his young visitors. "What can I do?" he sobbed.

"Hold on yet awhile," Rosa said.

"Remember, Topiltzin II, or whoever he is, came in peace. He has done no harm to anyone in this city. No cannon have been fired. He has acted as a man of peace," Peter said.

"I must go to my bed and rest."

When he left, Peter turned to Rosa. "What can we do? If the invader is indeed Topiltzin II and Montezuma has good reasons to believe it, it seems better to stay the course."

"I suppose." Rosa shrugged. "But I still wonder. Something tells me there's a lot going on here we don't know."

Chapter 13

⌒

A few days later, Topiltzin II approached Montezuma with a big smile. The children were with the emperor in the royal library, where the emperor sat going over his scrolls. "I have news for you," Topiltzin said. "I am leaving for Vera Cruz."

Montezuma sprang from his chair with great excitement and clasped Topiltzin's hand. "That is wonderful news, O most divine one! Will you be leaving to visit your emperor?"

"I cannot visit him right away. But I must make arrangements for the treaty we signed to be sent to him across the waters. The ship I arrived in is only suitable for the trip that brought me here from the nearby island of Cuba. I must find a way to make that ship sturdy enough for an ocean crossing. And by the way, you will never have to abandon your throne. The treaty we signed together is simply something I need to send the emperor so he knows I have visited you and that we have agreed to work together for the benefit of all the nations in the world."

Montezuma sank to his knees and kissed the god-warrior's feet. "Yes, yes, how wonderful! I have people in Vera Cruz who can help you build the ship you want. But I must warn you. It is important that you leave at this time. Many people here are rising up against you. They want you driven out, if not sacrificed."

Topiltzin nodded. "Yes, I understand. I am leaving for Vera Cruz tomorrow. My men in Vera Cruz will work with yours to build the ship that is needed for the long voyage."

Montezuma embraced him, tears of joy running down his cheeks. "In a way, I hate to see you leave. But it is best for all of us if you go."

"I may come back for a visit while the ship is being built. I am leaving a garrison of soldiers to protect you should you be in danger while I am away." He turned to Peter and Rosa. "Do you wish to remain here until I return? I don't believe Vera Cruz will be a safe place for you to visit right now. When the ship is built, you may want to board it for the land across the sea."

"Don't worry about us," Peter said. "Besides, we believe it is our duty to stay here with Montezuma. We will wait further instructions from—How shall I put it?—your father in heaven."

The god-warrior nodded with a smile. "Yes, my father—and yours."

Chapter 14

~~

When Topiltzin and the bulk of his troops crossed the Tacuba causeway and marched in the direction of Vera Cruz, many of the people in Tenochtitlan and around the lake were relieved. "He is leaving, just as we wish. The small garrison he left behind will not pose a threat to us, even with their magical shooting power. When the ship is built, he will sail across the sea and, all the gods willing, we will never see him again," Montezuma assured everyone.

And so the fear of war was set aside. Peter and Rosa continued to go out on the streets and canals as they pleased. But they were a little worried about the changing moods of Alvarado, the captain Topiltzin had put in charge of the garrison. He was brash and nervous and easily provoked. Peter and Rosa saw that Alvarado was suspicious of all the Mexicans around them. He suspected the aides of Montezuma who came to the palace to deliver messages or perform various services for the emperor. "I don't like those messengers with their big spears. If you ask me, they are up to no good. And when I see squads of Aztec soldiers passing our palace on the street, I can't help but think they are waiting for the right moment to attack us. They are animals, I tell you, not human. I think we have to keep our cannons ready to strike at them before they strike us. And when you come right down to it, I'm not sure we can trust Montezuma."

Alvarado was tall and gaunt, with a long, drooping face. He tended to pace up and down the halls a lot. Peter and Rosa were afraid he would blow his top any minute and bring all of Mexico down on them. But he was captain of the garrison, and the soldiers had been trained to obey him.

A few weeks after Topiltzin II had gone away, a centennial music festival dedicated to the triumphs of Smoking Mirror in the last hundred years took place in the courtyard opposite the palace where the garrison was stationed. Hearing the music, Peter and Rosa ran outside to see it. They were charmed by the beautiful costumes of the dancers, their colorful mantles and jewels of jade, damask, and ebony. They danced beautifully, and the gathered crowd was enchanted by their performances. Musicians blew on wooden flutes, beat on drums, and strummed marimbas.

"Oh, how I wish I could dance like that." Rosa nudged Peter.

"So do I," Peter said.

Then many among the spectators went out into the courtyard and began dancing with one another.

"Would you like to dance with me?" Rosa asked Peter, smiling in a very inviting way.

Peter was happily swept away with the dancers and found himself in the arms of Rosa, his face inches away from hers. Yes, Pauline Fishbinder, the famed beauty of their high-school class, was a plastic doll compared to Rosa, whose facial expressions radiated a vibrant beauty. They danced cheek to cheek. For the first time in his life, Peter had an inkling of what it would be like to enjoy the pleasures of heaven.

Suddenly, he heard a shot that could only have come from a musket. Then he saw a cannon ball fall into the keyboard of the marimba. Shouts and screams were heard everywhere. The crowd scattered, and Mexican soldiers appeared. Dozens of spears were thrown in the direction of the palace. Seven soldiers firing muskets from the balcony were struck down by javelins.

"Peter, what happened?" Rosa cried.

"It's that crazy Alvarado. He ordered those shots fired," Peter said. "We'd better run back into the palace."

"I hope Topiltzin comes back soon."

"That may not make things better."

The children ran into the palace doorway, which was opened for them and then bolted shut. Montezuma spoke to the angry mob from the balcony and appeared to calm them down. But Peter and Rosa knew that Alvarado had intensified the growing resentment the Mexicans felt about the unwanted visitors. Much worse, he had set off feelings of anger and distrust toward Montezuma himself.

Chapter 15

~⁓)

A few days later, news came that Topiltzin II was coming back to Tenochtitlan with a much larger military force than the one he had left with. He was approaching the causeway that led to the city from Tacuba. Learning of this, the lords of Smoking Mirror withdrew all forces from Tacuba and its surroundings. "We will leave the causeway open and undefended," Lord Maize Cob announced as he met with priests and lords in the city. "Let Topiltzin and his new army feel free to cross the causeway at will. When he arrives at the palace, we will attack him."

"You would attack a god? The god who gave us authority over all of Mexico?" Montezuma protested forlornly. He had invited Peter and Rosa to accompany him to the meeting.

"Exactly. O mighty Montezuma, you are right that the commander of foreign forces invading our land is the second coming of Quetzalcoatl Topiltzin. That is all the more reason why we should drive him away just as Smoking Mirror did in his last incarnation."

"But you are acting without my permission. I am the emperor. According to all the laws of our nation, my orders must be obeyed."

Lord Maize Cob and a few others wagged their heads when they heard this. "We have news for you, Your Excellency. Those of us who are members of the council, the very ones who gave you authority years ago, have met in conference. May we go with you into your private chambers to inform you of our recent decision?"

When the lords went inside with Montezuma, Rosa turned to Peter. "Topiltzin II is walking into a trap. We must warn him."

"Yes," Peter agreed. "The causeway to Tacuba is over a mile long. We must run as fast as we can. I'm sure I can do it in less than ten minutes. Why don't you wait here? Remember, I had all that hero training in Tollan I and can run far and fast. You wouldn't be able to keep up."

"Are you kidding? I'll race you, Mr. Super Kid. On your mark, let's go!"

They set aside their knapsacks and started out, running across canal bridges until they reached the broad causeway that led to Tacuba. The causeway was traffic free. They completed their run (Peter allowing Rosa to sprint ahead of him in the last several yards) just in time for the arrival of Topiltzin. They were amazed to see their friend at the head of a much larger military force than the one he had set out with. He had left with a few hundred men and was returning with an army of over thirteen hundred men, ninety-six horses, eighty musketeers, a hundred or so bowmen, and twenty cannon. Many of his new recruits were Mexican natives, but others had pale faces and were dressed in the uniforms of his soldiers. The mighty Topiltzin, astride his favorite horse, was smiling as he dismounted to greet his young friends with a big hug.

"How nice of you to come all this way to greet me," he said.

The youngsters were out of breath, but Rosa managed to speak up. "We came to warn you, your lordship," she said. "You are walking into a trap. The causeway is deserted, free of military guards or traffic of any kind, just to make it easy for you to come into the city. Then, when you don't expect it, they will attack you."

Topiltzin patted their shoulders and laughed. "Not as long as Montezuma backs me up. He is the emperor. They would not dare defy him. After all, he gets all his authority from my father."

"I don't know," Rosa went on. "Montezuma may not be able to help you as he once did. The priests of Smoking Mirror are rousing the people against him as well."

"But I have come with volunteers from Vera Cruz and Tabasco. I have volunteers from Cuba, including pale faces who serve the great emperor across the sea. As we speak, a ship outfitted by Cuban naval engineers is crossing the ocean, bearing the treaty Montezuma and I signed to the emperor. Things are looking good. Montezuma will be happy to know we can all work together to build a greater nation here in Mexico. Now my litter is ready. Climb aboard!"

Rosa whispered to Peter, "I wonder why he came with so many new soldiers?" Peter shrugged.

Peter and Rosa pulled themselves up into the litter and sat with Topiltzin. As they began to cross the causeway, they described the dancing festival and how Alvarado had fired upon the dancers thinking they had plans to attack the palace and kill everybody inside.

Topiltzin threw up his hands. "How stupid of him. The dancers were simply celebrating one of their holidays. I have learned that there are many holidays in this country, all of them religious and celebrated in peace. I shall have to discipline Alvarado and take away his authority. Everyone knows that Montezuma is living in that palace. I can't believe the people would want to do him any harm."

When they arrived in Tenochtitlan, the streets were deserted. They entered the palace of Face of Waters and were surprised to find that Montezuma was not waiting to greet them. A servant informed them that the emperor was secluded in a back room and wanted to speak to Topiltzin privately. "Do you want us to wait here?" Peter asked him.

Topiltzin stroked his beard thoughtfully. "I will ask the servants to find rooms for the new troops. But I think it is best if you two come with me. After all, Montezuma knows you are messengers sent by Quetzalcoatl, my father. If you are seen in my company, my position among the gods is more secure." He nodded his head and then frowned. "But there's something very wrong going on here. We must find out what it is."

They entered the inner sanctum with drapes celebrating the coronation of Montezuma hanging from the walls. One bore the image of the plumed serpent flying in the skies. They found Montezuma looking very sad. He embraced Topiltzin warmly, but his eyes were wet with tears. "These are bad times," he said. "I must tell you that I no longer have the power to serve you as you so deserve."

Topiltzin straightened up and smiled. "But I come with good news. Your empire is being joined with that of him who serves the God of creation. It is only a matter of time before our treaty is in his hands and he puts his own name on it. Together with him, we will build a greater Mexico, one that will be seen as a blessing to all the world."

Montezuma fought back tears and shook his head. "I must tell you—" He choked on his words and finally blurted out, "I am no longer the emperor of Mexico."

"But you are, and I am here to prove it. You sit on the throne I gave you."

"It matters not what you say or do. I am no longer the emperor, and the new emperor has ordered your destruction and that of your army."

"How is that possible?" Topiltzin took a step back as if the floor he stood on was no longer steady.

"A council of lords and priests was held just a few days ago. It is the same council that declared me emperor several years ago. At the time, it was wise to hail me as the divinely appointed heir to your throne. But now, the majority of lords and priests say that we owe our allegiance to Smoking Mirror. It is to him that we owe our success as a great empire. So now a new emperor has been appointed."

"But the people, the citizens of this city and of those around the lake, do they not honor me as the founder of this empire?" Topiltzin said.

Suddenly, a growing sound of voices shouting was heard coming from outside. "Do you hear that din?" Montezuma tried to stand up straight. "Those are the voices of the people. Yes, many honor you; some even love you. Many others are listening to the priests and lords, who tell them that you want to destroy our city. Do you hear them? They are the people of Tenochtitlan. There are thousands of them outside this palace demanding that you be delivered to them. I fear they wish to take my life as well."

"But that is impossible. These people adore you. I have witnessed it. I'm sure that if you step out on that balcony and speak to them in that wonderful way you have of inspiring people, they will end their shouting. Their confidence in you will be restored."

Montezuma shook his head in disagreement and then looked up at Topiltzin in sorrow. "I find that hard to believe, but you are my master. If it is the last thing I do on earth, it is my duty to obey you."

"But do be careful, your eminence," Peter and Rosa spoke up, looking up at the distressed emperor.

"My soldiers will hold up shields to protect you from violent acts," Topiltzin said.

Montezuma called out to servants from within. Three servants appeared, bowing and scraping their sandaled feet on the tiled floor.

"I am about to make a speech to the people," the emperor announced. "Prepare me in full royal dress." The servants went inside and immediately returned with the finest garments. They dressed the emperor in a pale-blue robe with golden embroidered flaps around the sleeves and neck; a jeweled crown with long, drooping feathers; a jade necklace; and jade earrings.

In such regal attire, the emperor went out on the balcony accompanied by Priest Scribe of Scrolls and a half-dozen armed soldiers. He was greeted by a mix of loud cheers and boos. A huge crowd had gathered in the courtyard and on all surrounding streets. Peter, Rosa, and Topiltzin stood in the palace doorway, looking on.

Montezuma stretched out an arm until the shouting died down.

Then he began to speak. "Fellow citizens, as you all know, I am no longer the emperor of our great and wonderful empire." This statement was received with a mix of protests and cheers.

"I have served as your emperor for many years, working to guide our empire when many of you were small children and before some of you were born. But as I step down, stripped of my powers by the lords who serve the gods who gave us the greatest empire the world has ever seen, I ask you one question. Who gave me the right to be your emperor when I first ascended to the royal throne? Who gave me the right to lead you all through the greatest time in our history? Some of you may know that my right to the throne was given to me by the god Quetzalcoatl. His son once held it and vowed to return to us one day. But that is only part of the answer. My right to the throne, the right of any emperor, comes from all of the gods working in harmony with him to create the proper balance of nature and the good of humankind."

These words were received in total silence. Montezuma went on. "Each god has his role to play, and his wishes must be served in accordance with the wishes of the others. Tlaloc is the god of rain. We need rain to grow our crops, but we also need the god of the sun to give us light and fire. Smoking Mirror has been good to us. He is the god of war and death. Certainly, all of us must die, and we all want to die nobly and with little pain. As for war, it is sometimes necessary but must always be used as a last resort. And so it is up to Quetzalcoatl to forge the necessary balance that prevents wars from leading to needless human suffering. For this, we must thank the god who granted me my throne, Quetzalcoatl Topiltzin!"

There was a thunderous reaction to these last words. Although there were cheers of approval, there were many more shouts of anger and disapproval. "Smoking Mirror made us great!" many shouted.

A mob rushed toward the palace, throwing spears, javelins, and rocks. Three of the soldiers guarding Montezuma were knocked down. As they fell, the emperor was struck by a flurry of rocks. Several hit him. A big one thrown with great force struck his head, and he fell. Blood gushed from his face and other parts of his body.

Of those who ran to his aid, Rosa was the first, followed by Peter. "Oh father," Rosa cried, kneeling before him and cradling his head in her lap. "Yes, you have always been like a father to me, and I love you."

The surviving soldiers carried Montezuma into the palace, where he was taken to his bedroom and laid to rest. He seemed to be suffering from severe shock. He refused to eat food and protested when Topiltzin's nurse dressed his wounds.

After all efforts to cure him failed, those who attended him became certain that Montezuma was dying. On what turned out to be his last visit, Topiltzin II promised to look after Montezuma's three young daughters and see that they married suitable noblemen from the land beyond the sea.

Montezuma died within a few days. Topiltzin wept for him as did the children and all the soldiers and servants who had come to love him. "Those of us who knew him well came to regard him as our father," Bernal, Topiltzin's chief officer, said. Peter and Rosa were quick to agree.

"A great and noble man," Topiltzin said, giving his eulogy. "A man learned and wise who not only governed his country with responsibility but dedicated himself to making the world a better place for all of humankind."

PART II

Chapter 16

W hen Topiltzin II delivered the body of Montezuma to the priests for burial, he was met with tears and cries of grief. But within the hour, a hostile crowd gathered in front of the palace, shouting and hurling showers of spears, arrows, and stones up at the balcony. "You have murdered our emperor!" many called out. "Death to you all!"

Topiltzin organized his troops and comrades in an effort to fight their way out of the city but quickly saw that it was impossible. The attacking forces seemed to be coming from everywhere. The conquistadors, Topiltzin's forces, were losing both men and arms. At Topiltzin's command, they retreated to the palace.

"Our powder is in danger of running low, and we are out of food and water," Bernal reported to his chief after they bolted the gate. "Thanks to the blunders of Alvarado, the muskets and cannon we had stored here were taken away from us. The Aztecs also took away many of our horses. All we have to defend ourselves with are the things you brought with you from Vera Cruz."

"They will have to do." Topiltzin shook his head ruefully. "When the crowd calms down, we will surge."

"How can they blame us for killing Montezuma when they are the ones who killed him?" Rosa said dolefully. "His faith in you as the god-king was our last hope."

"Don't speak like that, Rosa," Topiltzin said, caressing her affectionately. "Whether or not I am a god-king is of no help to us now. Yet we have hope. We have faith. I have faith in our brave troops. Beyond that, I have faith in the righteousness of our cause."

"And I have faith in you, Topiltzin," Peter said. "And if that cause brings an end to human sacrifice, I have faith in the cause."

At that moment, Priest Scribe of Scrolls, who had served Montezuma during his captivity in the palace, spoke up. "We must all have faith," he said. "Yes, your holiness, the raging crowd will calm down. They are just a mob letting off steam. Within the hour, they will go back to their homes. Your real threat is coming from Cuitlahuic, the new emperor. I have it on good authority that his army will attack us early tomorrow morning. In the meantime, they are destroying the bridges on the causeway that links us to Tacuba. I advise you to make your escape before too much damage is done."

Topiltzin slapped his forehead. "Destroying the bridges? How can we escape with all our artillery, our heavy armory, our horses?" He stroked his beard, deep in thought. "I faced a situation like this many years ago. How much time do we have? The only thing we can do is build a portable bridge and carry it out to fill the gaps in the causeway they created when they destroyed the bridges."

He slapped his forehead again, harder this time. "But how can we build a portable bridge here in this palace? Where do we get the materials? How would we get a portable bridge out of the palace? I don't see how." He dropped his hands to his sides, crestfallen.

"Topiltzin, your honor," Rosa said. "Something tells me Montezuma would know how to do it. This is the palace of his father, Face of Waters, right? Surely they must have had this same problem years ago. They knew it might happen to them, and so they came up with a solution. I'm sure they found a way."

"Of course!" Priest Scribe of Scrolls broke into a smile. "Now that you mention it, I believe they did." The priest suddenly called out to an elderly servant who was standing by. "I say, old man, do you recall any such thing?"

The old man scratched his head, and then his eyes lit up. "Why, yes. I believe they did build such a bridge. Yes, it still lies in one of the inner courtyards, one that hasn't been used in years. Follow me."

They trooped through gateways leading to other courtyards until they beheld what appeared to be a massive stack of wooden planks. It was at least twenty feet long, ten feet wide, and over ten feet high. The planks were bound by rubber straps. Other straps hung from either end.

"The straps on the ends are to be attached to the posts set along the causeway," the servant said. "That's what makes it a bridge."

"Perfecto!" Topiltzin exclaimed, his face brightening. "But will we have trouble getting the bridge out of the palace?"

"No, the archways are wide enough, and you know the gates to the outside will be wide enough when opened."

Chapter 17

~

A nd so, a little after midnight, with the moon rising over the lake, the great escape began. The remaining army of conquistadors, wearing heavy metal armor and carrying weapons, left the palace and set out for the causeway to Tacuba. They were accompanied by rebel warriors from Tabasco and Vera Cruz as well as Aztec servants and Tlaxcalan laborers who carried the portable bridge.

As they began the trek across the causeway, Topiltzin was positioned in the center of the formation, accompanied by Doña Marina, Doña Luisa, the daughters of Montezuma, and the children. The elite guard who carried the cannon marched directly behind them. Many troops marched behind the guard. The bearers of the portable bridge marched ahead of Topiltzin and other troops. Just as the entire formation was stretched out on the causeway, trumpets blared, whistles blew, and the mighty Mexican army charged from Tenochtitlan.

That the causeway was narrow was an advantage for Topiltzin's forces. The Mexican army pursuing them had to advance in a thin file.

Suddenly, the fleeing army was besieged by arrows, spears, and stones hurled at them from canoes sailing in the lake alongside the causeway. As the causeway was at least ten feet higher than the water level, the effect of this rain of weapons was limited. However, many of Topiltzin's troops were hit, sometimes seriously.

Then the worst thing happened. After Topiltzin, riding in the middle of his army on his horse, crossed the portable bridge, which had been lowered to fill a gap, Mexicans, rising from their canoes, clambered aboard it. They severed its connection with the causeway, ripped apart the rubber supports, hacked the planks to pieces with their hatchets, and scattered the remains into the lake.

Topiltzin's forces were now split in two. Half of his army and all his artillery were left on the Tenochtitlan side of the gap, easy victims for the Mexicans there, who were bearing down on them.

Topiltzin, astride his horse, turned to gaze at his stranded warriors in horror. "We must try to save them," he shouted to Bernal, who came running up to him. "We must do something," Topiltzin cried out to his devoted aide.

Bernal gave him a bewildered look. "It is out of the question, your lordship."

He sighed; Bernal was right. Yet he wasn't ready to accept the massacre of half his army. They would be slaughtered, some of them imprisoned to await blood sacrifice. Was there any way to save them?

At the same time, Topiltzin knew he couldn't expose his troops on the Tacuba side to more danger than they were already in. Hordes of canoeists were already attacking them, showering them with spears and stones. Some Aztecs were climbing the ropes that hung from posts on the causeway and hurling spears at the conquistadors, who fired back with the few weapons they had.

Taking a few steps to the edge of the gap and looking back on the city with its rising towers and teeming citizenry, Topiltzin was frozen with indecision. Peter and Rosa, standing thirty yards away on the free side, watched their commander with nervous excitement.

"Come on, Topiltzin, come to us!" they called out together.

"He's worried about his friends being stranded," Rosa said, clutching Peter's arm.

"What can he do? If he stays where he is, they'll kill him for sure."

"Look! I see them coming to him in their canoes. Peter, we must save Topiltzin!"

"Yes, he saved our lives, but how—"

Just then, javelins, knives, and rocks flew up at the horseback conquistador. As Rosa and Peter ran toward him, a rock struck his head, and he fell into the lake. The horse, whinnying, raced in the direction of Tacuba, passing the teenagers, who were sprinting to the place where Topiltzin had fallen. When they got there, they saw that the canoeists, presumably thinking Topiltzin dead, had turned back toward Tenochtitlan to aid their comrades in capturing the conquistadors stranded there.

Peter and Rosa looked over the side of the causeway to the lake, which was ten feet below them. They saw the body of Topiltzin face down and floating. Blood was streaming down his head and the back of his neck.

"He doesn't seem to be trying to swim," Peter said. "If he's not already dead, he's drowning."

"Come on, Peter. We jumped into the subfreezing pool of creation. This is just a country club swimming pool compared to that."

"Not quite, but take my hand," Peter said. Together, they leaped off the causeway and plunged into the lake. The water was cold but nowhere near the low temperature of the water during their swim in Tollan I.

"Is he dead?" Rosa asked as Peter reached the stricken Topiltzin and turned him over.

"I hope not, but he will be if we can't keep his head above water and get him out of here. Get on the other side. I'll keep his head up and paddle with one arm while you paddle on your side."

Holding the commander up while paddling, they swam in the direction of Tacuba, struggling to keep moving while holding aloft the great weight of their ironclad captain.

"I wish we could get this metal vest off him," Rosa said, grappling with the metal buttons.

Just then, they looked back to see a few distant canoes coming toward them.

"Those canoes are moving much faster than we are, and they're less than fifty yards off," Peter said. "If there was only some way we could climb up to the causeway—but there's nothing to hold on to."

Suddenly, a group of soldiers appeared on the edge of the causeway, looking down at them. They plunged into the water, relieving the teenagers of the heavy Topiltzin, and then helped Peter and Rosa climb a rope ladder suspended from a post on the last bridge connecting the causeway to Tacuba. Arrows and spears flew up at them as they climbed, but once on the bridge and behind its hardwood railing, the weaponry couldn't easily reach them. The soldiers fired down on the handful of canoes that turned back toward Tenochtitlan.

Rosa, demonstrating her Junior Red Cross training, applied artificial respiration, pressing her hands down on Topiltzin's stomach until spurts of water blew out of his mouth. Finally, the great commander's eyes opened. He raised himself up slowly, belching, and finally broke into a big smile. Two soldiers ran to support him. They slowly lifted him until he stood straight up between them. Cheers went up from all the surviving troops.

For all the cheering, the troops were a pitiful sight to see. Their clothing was all in tatters. Many of them were wounded and had to be held up by comrades. They had lost most of their artillery. Many muskets had been lost, and it turned out their supply of ammunition was low. Doña Marina and Doña Luisa ran up to kiss the commander. Others ran up to shake his hand. He raised a hand to quiet them while he spoke.

"Comrades, my fellow conquistadores, hear me." He summoned Rosa and Peter to stand beside him. "I have been raised from the dead by two angels sent to me from heaven. And so I know that our mission has been blessed by God. Yes, we have lost over half of our dedicated comrades. Many of our brothers are dead or imprisoned in the very island we escaped from. As you know, we have lost our good friend Montezuma. We have suffered a defeat today. But we have lost none of our courage, our belief in the righteousness of our cause, or our will to continue the good fight!

"So I say to you, my brave and valiant comrades, we must retreat today, but on my life, I swear to you we will return to this place in the very near future and achieve a glorious conquest. Now on to Tacuba!"

Chapter 18

Topiltzin expected the Aztecs to pursue him and his forces through the streets of Tacuba. To his surprise, he and his battered army met with little resistance as they passed through Tacuba and beyond. Deserted plains and distant mountains appeared before them.

"What happened to the Aztec army?" Topiltzin asked Lord Chief of Scribes, who continued to serve him.

"They have other priorities," the scribe explained. "Their first duty is to Smoking Mirror. Before they can even consider pursuing you, they must sacrifice those in captivity to the god of war. That is bad news for your lost comrades, but it gives you and the rest of us a chance to escape."

Topiltzin winced, and so did Rosa and Peter standing by. "How awful! This is true barbarism. All my good comrades, my friends."

"I don't think Montezuma would have allowed that," Rosa said tearfully.

"Would he have had a choice?" Topiltzin said. He and Peter shook their heads sorrowfully. Then Topiltzin straightened his bearing and looked ahead at the distant mountains. "Terrible, terrible, but we must press on."

"Where do we go now, captain?" Bernal asked.

"We must go where we can get help. I'm not sure the Tlaxcalans will be happy to see us, but we must go to them and seek their alliance. They may find it to their advantage to join us in an all-out fight against their enemies, the Aztecs. We will march straight to Tlaxcala by way of Otumba, which is on the other side of the mountain range just ahead of us."

The army marched for six days, crossing the steep mountain pass by which they had descended on their first visit to Tenochtitlan. Peter and Rosa trekked right along with them.

When they reached the plain of Otumba, they were stunned to find themselves confronted by a large military force led by the Aztec commander, Serpent Master, whom Topiltzin, Bernal, and others recognized. Topiltzin, who had been wounded in the head and in his left hand, was suffering from pain and weariness. Yet he summoned up the will to meet the surprising threat head-on.

He called up his horsemen and ordered them to charge the leading Aztec officers, who could be easily identified by their splendid uniforms—their plumes, the banners attached to their backs, and their jeweled headdresses in the form of serpents.

Acting swiftly, the Mexicans attacked them on all sides. But just as the defeat of the crippled conquistadors seemed certain, Topiltzin and his aide, Juan Salamanca, came face-to-face with Serpent Master himself. He was wearing rich gold armor with silver plumes and was wielding a huge volcanic-glass club.

Topiltzin charged, and his horse struck Serpent Master on the side. At the same time, Juan de Salamanca stabbed him with his lance. The captain general fell. Salamanca took his club away from him as Serpent Master bled to death. And then, to the astonishment of Topiltzin and his comrades, the Mexican army, seeing the death of their leader, stopped fighting and hastily retreated.

"What in the world?" Bernal and his aides gave one another puzzled looks.

After all the Mexicans had left the field of battle, Priest Scribe of Scrolls offered his interpretation of what had happened. "Your

Excellency, the killing of their leader was taken by his troops as a sign that you are indeed Quetzalcoatl Topiltzin and Montezuma was right. It was a mistake to try to overcome you by force. To kill you would indeed bring about a war of all the gods and destroy the world."

"So we have to thank Montezuma for saving the day." Rosa threw out her chest proudly.

"Very good, Rosa, but I like to think Juan Salamanca and I had just a little something to do with it," Topiltzin said with a grin.

As night fell, the weary conquistadors gathered for their meager supper of maize and the flesh of one of their horses killed in battle. "We are within a day or so of crossing the Tlaxcalan frontier," Topiltzin said, looking at the hills ahead of them bathed in moonlight. "I don't know if they will be friendly or will attack us. We are very weak. Bernal tells me our numbers at this time are 440 men, 20 horses, 12 crossbows, and 7 muskets. We have no powder, and our men are covered with wounds."

But on the very next morning, a group of nobles from the Tlaxcalan federation arrived with friendly greetings. They all embraced with much weeping on both sides. The Tlaxcalans grieved for the losses the conquistadors had suffered and promised to care for them. They all left for Tlaxcala, where the soldiers' wounds were treated and all enjoyed a bountiful feast.

Chapter 19

〜

It wasn't long before the Tlaxcalan Council of Four, the governing body of Tlaxcala, voted to support the conquistadors' invasion of Tenochtitlan. Since it was being led by Quetzalcoatl Topiltzin, the rightful heir of the Aztec empire, the council felt such an invasion was bound to succeed. Topiltzin promised that all those who supported him would win freedom from having to pay tribute to the Aztecs in the form of victims for human sacrifice. Instead, they would gain prosperity as well as basic human rights. The council said they would begin by providing a well-trained army of over ten thousand men. They would then enlist military forces from neighboring states suffering from the control of the Aztecs.

Meanwhile, Peter and Rosa enjoyed the pleasures to be found in the city of Tlaxcala. People were friendly. The market offered many treats. There were shops filled with sparkling jewelry and beautiful handmade crockery. Other outdoor shops were brimming over with tangy fruit and fresh vegetables.

At the same time, Peter experienced undercurrents of fear that grew with each day he and Rosa spent in Tlaxcala. He heard rumors from troops that the new rulers of Tenochtitlan, who were increasing their demands on their vassal states and aware of the threat to their power in Tlaxcala, might invade the rebel state before Topiltzin organized the forces he needed. Walking the streets with Rosa at his side, Peter found himself more concerned for her welfare than his own. But either way, should Topiltzin invade Tenochtitlan, thousands of people would be killed in the battle. Peter thought that maybe he should ask Topiltzin to allow Rosa to stay in Tlaxcala. But that might be dangerous as well. Of course, Quetzalcoatl had warned them in the beginning that he was sending them on a dangerous mission and they could back out if they so wished. But Rosa had said loudly and clearly that she was up for it.

At the end of a week, Topiltzin announced that he was ready to invade Tenochtitlan. The Tlaxcalans had amassed a huge, eager and willing fighting force from neighboring vassal states who wanted to throw off the yoke of the Aztecs. Since the death of Montezuma, the Aztecs had doubled their demands for sacrificial victims so that more cities were now willing to revolt. The Tlaxcalans were confident that Topiltzin would gain more allies along the way to Tenochtitlan.

Meanwhile, messengers from Vera Cruz brought word that many ships from Cuba containing well-armed soldiers, horses, powder, and guns had arrived, ready for combat. Then came the best news of all! A large ship had arrived from Spain carrying troops and artillery.

On the eve of setting out on his massive invasion, Topiltzin spoke with Peter and Rosa. "There's going to be some fierce fighting," he announced. "Tens of thousands of people will be killed. Montezuma was right. It will be the end of the world as we know it. But I have confidence that a new and better world will come in its place."

"The fighting will be awful," Rosa said. "But with more and more tribes and people from Spain and Cuba wanting to join you, it seems that victory will be yours for sure."

"I don't see how you can lose," Peter said, ready to plead for Rosa's safety.

Topiltzin smiled and ran his hands through the hair of his young friends. "Everything seems to be on our side. But mind you, if the invasion of Tenochtitlan should succeed as many now believe, future historians must tell it as it happened. The war was won not by this invasion but long before, when everything looked hopeless. It was won by the courage of my comrades and by the two of you. You turned everything around. You saved my life when it seemed almost certain that I was a dead man floating. And if we should now claim victory in Tenochtitlan, let history take note. The war was won in the blood-soaked lake of Tetzcuco and on the windswept plain of Otumba. It was in those dark days that you and our army won the war for us."

Peter and Rosa nodded pensively, and Topiltzin gave them big hugs. "But now, for the battle I am waging against Tenochtitlan, your services are not required. I don't believe you should go there with us. You would be risking your lives for no good reason. And doesn't Quetzalcoatl—my, uh, father in heaven—have another mission for you? I recommend that you go to Cholula, which will not be affected by the violence. It turns out Cholula has the best record against human sacrifice of all the places in this so-called new world. I can tell you that Cholula is the city where peace terms will be drawn when this war is over. Cholula is a day's journey by horse from here. I have left a dozen horses to be kept in stalls on the palace grounds here. I asked Chief Eagle Eyes to make one available to you should you ask."

"Oh, thank you," Peter and Rosa said together. Peter felt relieved that Rosa would not be brought to a war in which many people would lose their lives. He was also relieved that he didn't have to take part in it.

Topiltzin brought his deserving young comrades to his chest and hugged them. "Farewell, my angels. I go to war. You go to peace. Yours is the better cause."

Topiltzin kissed them both on the cheeks and, with a wave, turned from them and walked to the head of his strengthened army.

Rosa wept. Both she and Peter were sad to see their friend, whom they had come to admire and love, leave them. When he was out of their sight, they prayed together, Rosa leading the prayer. They prayed for Topiltzin's survival in the most important battle of his life. Although the children had come to believe that war must always be the last resort, they prayed that the outcome of this one would be good for the people of Mexico and all the world.

PART III

Chapter 20

～

That night, Peter and Rosa went early to their beds located in the back of the palace. Moonlight flowed through their bedroom window as they drifted into dreamland. They woke up with a start as a strong beam of light streamed through the window. They looked outside to see—yes, it was the god Quetzalcoatl himself, the plumed serpent, sliding down a laser beam toward their bedroom.

The serpent flew through the glass without breaking it and sat on his coils on the palace floor between the beds of the children.

"Good morning, sleepyheads," the serpent said, a small laugh giving a lilt to his otherwise solemn voice. "It's time to get up and set out on your next mission.

"If all goes well, it will be your last. Should you succeed, you will have passed all your tests and be able to receive your diploma."

"Our last mission!" Rosa sat up, her eyes glistening with expectation. "Where are we going?"

"You are going to Cholula, just as you expected. Not tomorrow, but twenty years in the future. The cosmic war will be over. Your mission will be to bring about a peace that will change the world."

"Change the world? Us teenagers change the world? That's a tall order!" Peter said.

"Not for you two." The serpent smiled, nodding his feathered head.

"You've done good work since the very beginning of your travels. You brought about peace between Tollan and the Maya. You won the ball game that prevented a war in Tollan II. And now you've helped Montezuma and the great warrior from across the sea come to an understanding, an understanding that prevented a war that would have been a much greater catastrophe than the one that is raging now."

"Tell me, O mighty plumed serpent," Rosa said. "You spoke of the great warrior from across the sea who befriended Montezuma. Is that great warrior the second coming of your son, Topiltzin, whom we knew in Tollan II and who told us he would come back in the next coil of time to reclaim his throne? Montezuma seemed to believe he was. He didn't look quite the same as the Topiltzin we knew, but well, it's been five hundred years, and he has a lot of the same ideas as the Topiltzin we knew. He wants to abolish human sacrifice, and he let on to us that he was the second coming of Topiltzin."

The serpent sighed deeply, lifted himself up on his coils, and settled down again. "He fooled you on that one. Actually, Montezuma fooled you after fooling himself. Then the great warrior, whose name happens to be Hernan Cortés, decided to play the part and fooled all of you."

"Hernan Cortés!" The children shouted together and looked at one another in astonishment. "That means what we are seeing *is*, in fact, the Spanish invasion."

"And this must be the year 1519," Rosa said. "But your son, Topiltzin. We knew him! We heard him say he was going to return in one coil of time, which is now, to reclaim his throne. What happened to him?"

Quetzalcoatl looked down at the floor. His young disciples were surprised to see tears form in his eyes. "My son, my dear, beloved son," he said, his voice choking and his feathers flattening against his skin. "I have lost my son. He left his home in the stars many rounds of time ago. Where he went, I do not know. If he took human form again, which he must have done, he died, as all humans do, several generations ago. Yet he may have gone to Spain, and if so, Hernan Cortés may very well be his descendant. "Indeed, my Topiltzin may be his great-great-great-grand-pappy," the serpent added with a sad smile.

"But now, to your final mission." The serpent raised his head. "I want you to go to Cholula. It is in Cholula that the new nation of Mexico will be born."

"We knew you would want us to go to Cholula, your holiness," Peter said, "as did your great-great-many-times-great grandson. He left a horse for us to ride to Cholula. We can be there tomorrow night."

"You won't need a horse to ride, and I don't want you there tomorrow. I want you there in the year 1540, twenty years from now. As you very well know, one of my feathers can get you there right away."

"What's so special about the year 1540?" Rosa asked.

"As I told you, that is the time and place where and when the new nation will be born. It all begins a few years earlier in a city lying in the mountains south of us. A bishop named Fray Bartolme de Las Casas is protesting, in sermons and in writings, the cruel treatment Native Americans are receiving from the overlords of New Spain. As a remedy for this, Las Casas wants to lift the ban on Spanish soldiers marrying native women. The reason for this ban is that the overlords believe the native women, as well as the native men, are dumb brutes, animals without souls. For a Spanish soldier to marry one of them would be the same as marrying a pig or a goat.

"Bartolme will argue that lifting this ban is the only way that a new nation, sharing the best values of both races, can be formed."

"Wow," Peter and Rosa said together. "That's neat!" Rosa said. "Awesome!"

"I have received word from one of my spies, a quetzal bird, as you may very well guess, that the good bishop's pleas will come to the attention of the pope in Rome in the year 1537. As a result, the pope will deliver a statement known as a Papal Bull. In this statement, the pope will declare that the native people of America are not dumb brutes but human beings having souls and should be welcomed into the folds of the Church."

"Wonderful!" the children exclaimed together. "That means the Spanish soldiers can marry the native women," Rosa said.

Quetzalcoatl held up a cautious finger. "It would seem that way. You would think the good bishop will win his case. But there are problems—big problems. Solving these problems is the reason I want to send you there."

"Solving the problems? Us?" Peter and Rosa looked at one another in awe and then looked back at Quetzalcoatl.

The serpent paused and shook his head sadly. "In the next several years, more and more conquistadors will come to view the natives of these parts as less than human. No God-fearing soldier of the king's army will even consider marrying and definitely will not be permitted to marry one of them. In Cholula, the commander who will soon order this ban against Spaniards marrying native Americans is Luis Alvarado."

"Alvarado?" Rosa fairly leaped up from her bed. "We know him! He's a very bad person!"

"He killed many Mexicans outside our palace in Tenochtitlan just because they were dancing," Peter said.

"And he called them animals," Rosa said. "I thought Topiltzin, or Cortés as you call him, had him fired."

"Apparently, he will be able to pay off other commanders when Cortés is retired to Spain," Quetzalcoatl said with a shrug.

"But what can we do?" Peter asked.

The serpent raised himself up and then settled down again on his coils. "I have been informed that Alvarado will receive a copy of the Papal Bull sent to Cholula and will not share it with the troops under his command. My loyal quetzal bird, having won the confidence of one of Alvarado's servants, has so notified me."

"Shame!" Rosa said.

"It's just like him," Peter said.

Quetzalcoatl nodded in agreement. "Now to get you started on your mission. I want you to take a feather that will light up on my coat in just a minute. I am sending you to Cholula in the year 1540. As I have tried to explain, Cholula has been the place where groups in Mexico have come together to settle their differences for hundreds of years. As Cholula goes, so goes the nation. Your mission? Love and marriage between the Spaniards and the natives. Bring them together in Cholula, and you will be giving birth to a new world."

"Awesome!" Rosa gasped.

"But how do we do that?" Peter said.

"That is for you to decide. You have been given all the training and experience you need. This is your biggest and your final mission. All right? Watch my coat. Do you see the feather light up? Good. It is your ticket to Cholula. The fate of the new world is in your hands."

Rosa plucked the feather and took Peter's hand. Everything in the room began to spin. Suddenly, they were up in the sky, looking down on mountains and valleys. Everything began to blur, until, still twirling, they descended toward earth and came to rest on the largest pyramid ever built by humankind.

Chapter 21

⁓

To their surprise, when Peter and Rosa landed on the top of the pyramid, they found themselves standing in the courtyard of a beautiful white church. Four towers from which red steeples rose crowned the building. In the distance, the children could see the volcano Popocatepetl billowing plumes of smoke that stretched out for miles. On the doorstep of the church, a young native woman sat weeping. She was lovely, with large, dark eyes and lustrous black hair streaming over her shoulders. She wore a white blouse embroidered with images of roses. A red sash was wrapped around her trim waist. A long, black cotton skirt flowed down to her ankles, and her small, well-formed feet were bare. She appeared to be in her early twenties. Her chin rested in her hands as tears streamed down her cheeks.

"Why are you crying, young lady?" Rosa asked in Nahuatl as Peter adjusted his language decoder.

"Young lady? I am no young lady. I am a savage beast, an animal. They tell me so—all the Spanish soldiers save one, the man I love and had hoped to marry."

"You are not a savage beast," Peter said. "You are a human, a lovely young woman and one of the most beautiful I have ever seen."

"And you speak Nahuatl, a human language, perfectly," Rosa said. "My father spoke it. He was a Mexican and a human as was my mother.

After all, they produced me, and I can also speak the language of the conquistadors as well as they do."

"Why are you sitting outside the church?" Peter asked. "Don't you want to go inside?"

"I am not allowed to go inside. They say I might run up to the altar and knock over the chalice, spilling the wine that is the blood of God, just like any dumb animal that has no respect for religion."

"Have you ever done those things?"

"How can I? They won't give me a chance to prove that I won't. They think the same about all us natives." She tried to hold back fresh tears but couldn't. "The chief commander in Cholula, Luis Alvarado, won't allow any of the soldiers under his command to marry one of us. He says that to do so is beneath the dignity of a soldier serving the crown of Spain. There was a priest here who wanted to perform the marriage ceremony for my fiancé and me. Alvarado drove him out of Cholula and is putting a priest more to his liking in his place."

"We know a few things about Alvarado," Rosa said. "He's as nasty as they come. But we are here to put an end to his crazy rules and will do everything we can to help you marry the man you love and who loves you. What is your name, by the way? I am Rosa, and this is Peter."

The young woman smiled, although tears continued to stream down her cheeks. "I am Sulma. Oh, thank you—you are both angels. But I don't think you can change Commander Alvarado. Once his mind is set on something, nothing can stop him."

Peter chuckled. "We have a plan. But your fiancé—What is his name? Where is he?"

The woman lifted her eyes as if the very mention of her beloved was a balm to her heart.

"His name is Francisco, Lieutenant Francisco Juarez. He is inside the church with two of his comrades."

"We'll go in and introduce ourselves," Rosa said to Peter.

The children entered the darkened church. The only light came from candles set along the side aisles and over the altar and from rays of sunlight drifting through stained-glass windows. Out of respect for the teachings of her childhood, Rosa dipped her hand in the basin of holy water set by the doorway. In the middle of the main aisle, not far from them, three young Spanish soldiers carried on a conversation in hushed tones. They wore hard leather vests over blousy pink-and-white shirts that reached down to the tops of their high leather boots. They held leather caps in their hands.

"But you see, Lieutenant Juarez, we can't possibly allow that beast, the one you call your girlfriend, in here," one of the soldiers said, patting his bulging stomach. He appeared to be the oldest of the three, and his stomach was a good testimony to his age. "God knows what she'd do. Why do we ban cats and dogs from going inside the church? Can't you just imagine them climbing up to the choir and joining the chorus with yowls of woof woof and meow meow? You can't trust any of these animals. This savage could run down the nave during a Mass, jump over the altar rail, attack the priest, the altar boys. Who knows? She might even use the sacristy as a bathroom. Can you imagine the stench?"

He laughed, giving his bulging stomach a shake. One of the other two soldiers, a man who was thin and balding, joined him. The third soldier, obviously the youngest, handsome and well-built, scowled at his companions.

"Comrades, you must know that my fiancée and any of her sisters would never do such things. Lieutenant Garcia, have you ever seen a woman in these parts act in the way you describe in any house of worship?"

Lieutenant Garcia rolled his eyes and nodded. "Not in their pagan temples where they worship idols. But this is a house of God. These savages have no respect for the one true God."

"Rather, you have no respect for my fiancée, the woman I love."

Lieutenant Garcia burst into laughter at these words. "Woman? Ho, ho! That's a good one. That little beast of yours who is half jaguar and half monkey, a woman? Oh, Please! Ha, ha, ha!" The others cautioned him to lower his voice.

At this point, Rosa and Peter approached the military officers and stood before them.

"How dare you call my sister a beast!" Rosa said, speaking fluent Spanish. "My mother was one of her race, and my mother brought me up to go to church every Sunday. The woman you have insulted is a human being who wants to get married in this church. She loves Lieutenant Juarez, and she loves the God you claim to worship, although she calls him by a different name. And by the way, the one who has no respect for this church is you, with all your loud laughing."

The officers were so taken aback by Rosa's scolding that they did not know how to respond.

Peter picked up the attack. "Lieutenant Garcia, if I have your name right, and you, sir." He pointed to the thin, balding officer. "What is your name, if I may ask?"

"Lieutenant Arturo Lopez," the officer replied, looking somewhat offended by the challenges presented by two children.

"Gentlemen," Peter went on, softening his voice. "Forgive me for saying this, but are you totally blind? Tell me the truth. Do you honestly believe that the lovely young woman who is crying outside this church is a savage beast? Just look at her. Is she not one of the most beautiful women you have ever seen in this part of the world or the world you come from? And does she not comport herself like a lady, full of poise and grace? Would you not consider it a great pleasure if she allowed you to take her hand and place your arm around her trim waist? Tell the truth!"

Lieutenant Garcia stifled a laugh but managed to give his beer belly a good shake. "I'll grant you she's cute, like a wild kitty cat. But I'm sure if I tried to steal a kiss, she'd scratch me with one of her claws."

"That proves she has good taste." Lieutenant Juarez smiled dryly.

Lieutenant Lopez grimaced and shook his head. "My boy," he said, addressing Peter, "I must confess that much of what you say is true. We have been taught by our commanders that these natives are all animals, in no way human. And yet I must admit on many a lonely night I wish

I had the company of such an animal as Francisco's fiancée. There is little for us to do here when we have finished our daily duties except play cards or maybe drink a little wine sent over from Spain. As I go to my bed, I'm always left with an empty feeling. Is this all there is? I have no idea when I will be sent home, if ever."

Suddenly, they all heard chanting sounds coming from somewhere outside the church.

"What's that sound? I hear a lot of shouting," Rosa said.

"Shouting, yes," Lieutenant Garcia answered her. "Shouting lies, cursing, slandering! Those sounds you hear are coming from the very savage beasts we were talking about. Why do our commanders let them run wild? We should have made slaves of them the way our countrymen have done with many of the black Africans. But Alvarado says you can't make a slave out of a savage beast. You can train a horse but not a jaguar. We must make examples of them. Kill their leader. I'll talk to Alvarado."

"Let's go out and see what's going on," Rosa said to Peter.

They ran out into the courtyard and joined Sulma, who was looking over the wall. Below them, at the foot of the pyramid, they saw a band of Cholulans dressed in raggedy clothes shouting and carrying posters with Nahuatl writing on them. They were not rowdy, however, but marched in an orderly way. A group of Spanish soldiers stood by, aiming rifles at the demonstrators, ready to fire at any sign of violence.

"What do the posters say? What are they shouting?" Peter asked Rosa. Then he heard a click in his head, and his language decoder switched to Nahuatl.

"You promised us freedom, prosperity, dignity. We are humans, not savages. We want freedom, respect. Freedom now!"

"Oh, Peter, let's go down there and talk to them," Rosa said. "Isn't it our job to help them gain what they want?"

"I have an idea," Peter said. "Look, do you see that engraved mural down near the bottom of the pyramid? It's big, above thirty feet long and twenty feet wide. See it? It's an image of Quetzalcoatl flying."

"Yes, I see it. It juts out from the wall about forty feet from the ground."

"It's been there for hundreds of years," Sulma said as Francisco joined them, taking Sulma's hand. She smiled, resting her cheek on his shoulder. "Yes, it is an image of the great god, Quetzalcoatl," Sulma went on. "I have knelt on the ground below and worshipped him ever since I was a little girl. So have all my people. It has been in the presence of Quetzalcoatl that we have settled the differences between us throughout our history."

"And did your leaders ever stand on the ledge above Quetzalcoatl's image to address the people?" Peter asked.

"Yes, years ago, but not since the Spaniards took over."

"Then it's time to revive one of the great traditions of Cholula," Peter said with a big smile. He turned to Rosa. "Rosa, why don't we go down and perch ourselves on that ledge that runs just above the sculpted Quetzalcoatl while we make our case to the people about love and marriage."

"Wonderful idea!" Rosa clapped her hands. "And should we bring Sulma with us?"

"That's the idea. And Francisco, do you know where that priest is, the one who wanted to perform your wedding and who Alvarado drove away?"

Francisco's eyes brightened. "Why, yes, he's staying in a village nearby. He's with some people I know."

"Good, go down and fetch him and tell him to be ready after Rosa and I speak to your comrades in arms. Don't worry about Alvarado. Rosa and I have a way to deal with him."

Francisco fairly leaped into the air. "Are you children, or are you angels?"

"I say they are angels." Sulma beamed.

Following their delegated angels, Sulma and Francisco began their descent down the long stairway that led to the bottom of the pyramid. Lieutenants Garcia and Lopez followed. "This should be good," Garcia said to his comrade, giving him a nudge with his elbow and smirking. "If I know Alvarado, these little brats, along with the she-devil and old Francisco himself, will be locked up in the stockade before sundown. Do I hear volunteers for the firing squad?" He erupted into more laughter.

When they reached the level of the engraved mural, the angels saw a path that led to it. "Look, Peter," Rosa said. "This path will take us to the ledge above Quetzalcoatl's mural. That ledge is wide enough for us to stand on."

"Good," Peter said. "Sulma, come with us. Francisco, by the time you come back with the priest, we should have the crowd on our side."

"You have inspired me," Francisco said. "Yes, you are angels! I shall return with Father Rodrigo."

Peter, Rosa, and Sulma set out on the dirt path, brushing aside plants that grew all around them. Beer-bellied Garcia and the sad-eyed Lieutenant Lopez walked behind Francisco to the bottom of the pyramid, where they joined the armed troops.

Chapter 22

~

The Cholulan protesters stopped their chanting and looked up in wonder as the children and Sulma assumed their positions on the ledge above the sacred mural. The soldiers looked up as well. There was a sudden silence and a stillness.

"Who are they?" cries went up. "Those little ones are dressed so strangely. Are they children? Are they angels?"

"Yes, angels," others uttered in hushed tones.

"And that woman," one of the soldiers said. "She is dressed like a Mexican, but she has the beauty of a princess."

"Who are you? What do you want of us?" an officer wearing the badge of a captain said.

"We come to you as friends. We want friendship with all Cholulans. Friendship, peace, and love! All hail Cholula!" Peter said.

Several voices from all sides cried out, "Cholula, Cholula! Peace and love!" Others among the natives cried out, "Peace and love exist here no more. We live as slaves, robbed of freedom and dignity!"

As they listened, the visitors and Sulma had a good view of the city of Cholula with its adobe houses, some with courtyards, and the Spanish houses with their red-tiled roofs, many with fountains in their courtyards. There were also ancient Mexican temples in the form of small pyramids set against a background of rolling green hills.

The crowd filled the square in front of the pyramid and surrounding streets. They were silent now, waiting to hear something from the visitors who seemed to have appeared before them from outer space.

"We come to help you reclaim your freedom and dignity, all of you, Mexicans and conquistadores," Rosa said. "Yes, conquistadores, we know that you have been robbed of your freedom and dignity as much as the people of Mexico whom you are appointed to watch over."

There was much stirring, hushed voices mingling with cries of both joy and fear below. "They must be angels!" several voices were heard to say. Then someone called up, "Tell us, O you angels, were you sent to us from heaven?"

"Well, you could say that," Peter said with a small shrug.

There was much applause from the Cholulans and scattered applause among the Spanish. "Then tell us if you have come to us with a message from heaven intended to guide us. What are we to do to win the rights that have been denied us, those of us who are conquistadores as well as those of us who are natives of this land known as Mexico," someone called out. Peter, Rosa, and Sulma recognized the voice of Lieutenant Juarez.

"Good question," Peter said. "Let me begin by speaking to those of you whose duty it is to maintain peace and help build a new country in this land. You know that most of you will be required to serve here for many years, quite possibly the rest of your lives. How many of you would like to marry a kind, loving woman and raise a family right here in Cholula?"

These words were greeted with silence. Then a few hands were raised. Finally, over half of the uniformed soldiers raised their hands and shouted, "Yes! We want to marry and raise a family here in Cholula!"

The delegated angels and Sulma applauded. "Just what we thought," Rosa said. "To begin with, you must throw off the blindfolds of prejudice that have been placed on you and look at things as they really are. You will see that there are many lovely women around you. Yet you are forbidden to marry them. Why is that?"

"We cannot marry them because they are savage beasts, animals!" Lieutenant Garcia called out. This comment was followed by grumbling from the Cholulans and dead silence from the rest of the military.

"Animals? Savage beasts?" Peter said, drawing Sulma to his side. Sulma blushed as all eyes were now fixed on her.

"Behold this woman!" Peter said. "Does she not have eyes, a nose, ears, a mouth, and a chin in the same places as any woman you have ever seen? Look at her skin, slightly reddish but perfectly smooth and silky. Behold the lovely curves of her figure that run all the way down to her small, pretty feet. You have seen her among you many times, just one in a crowd. And indeed, she is one of many lovely women who can be seen all around you. Yet you have paid no attention to her or her sisters because of the lies you have been told. So take a good look at this woman and look around you. Behold the women!"

"You men are more lucky than you know," Rosa said. "From where I stand, I can see there are more Cholulan women among you than there are Cholulan men. So there is much joy to spread around. Joy for Spaniards and joy for Cholulans of both sexes! So let's hear it for love and marriage! Love and marriage!"

There were many shouts of joy followed by silence and some groans and sighs of despair.

"I still say they are savage beasts," beer-bellied Garcia called out. "Why, they can't even speak a human language. The gobbledygook I hear them speak is nothing but monkey talk. I hear monkeys making the same nonsense sounds in the trees!"

This was followed by many boos from all sides.

"The language they speak is Nahuatl, the language Montezuma spoke," Rosa said. "Whatever you thought of him, he was no monkey. I can speak Nahuatl because my father taught it to me. It is a beautiful language. So listen to Sulma speak Nahuatl."

Sulma took Rosa's arm. "Rosa, I would like to speak to the soldiers in their language, Spanish. I have learned it from Francisco."

It seemed that all of Cholula was quiet as Sulma began. "*Saludos,*

senores. Por favor, quiero casarme con mi novio, Teniente Francisco Juarez.
El es un hombre muy bueno—guapo, amable, inteligente y bravo. Estoy
muy enamorado con el. Queremos hacer hijos y viven juntos siempre.
Gracias."

Listening to it on his decoder, Peter heard, "Greetings, ladies and
gentlemen. If you please, I would like to marry my fiancé, Lieutenant
Francisco Juarez. He is a good man—handsome, kind, intelligent, and
wonderful. I am very much in love with him. We hope to have children
and live with one another always. Thank you."

Sulma's words were received by applause from almost all of the
Spanish servicemen and many of the Cholulans who had learned some
Spanish during the occupation. The applause was followed by a long
silence.

At last, Lieutenant Lopez spoke up. "Many of us would be happy
to marry a native of these parts, and we agree with you angels that they
are lovely women. But we are under orders. Our commander-in-chief,
Luis Alvarado, has forbidden us to marry any of them. He says it would
be an act of perversion for any soldier of the respected and admired
Spanish army to marry a creature less than human. He asks us, 'Would
an honorable man marry a pig, a dog, a serpent?' You have made a good
case to the contrary, but we must obey Commander Luis Alvarado. He
is our authority."

"And where does Commander Alvarado receive his authority?"
Peter asked.

"He was commissioned by the military council in Tenochtitlan.
They gave him his authority."

"Is there a higher authority in the world you come from whose
orders could confirm or cancel the orders of Commander Alvarado?"
Peter asked.

After a silence, Lieutenant Lopez said, "Only the pope in Rome."

Rosa and Peter clapped their hands together. "Right on!" Rosa
exclaimed. "The pope in Rome! Well, we have news for you. You know
we came to you on a mission, right? Well, while we were way up in

heaven someplace, we met a little bird—call him the Holy Spirit—who let us in on a secret. Tell them, Peter."

"The holy spirit? A secret?" The crowd buzzed with excitement.

"Now hear this," Peter said. "The little bird, the Holy Spirit as Rosa said, told us that a message from the pope in Rome has been sent to all of you granting you the freedom to marry whomever you wish and invites you to get married in the church."

This time the cheering was thunderous. Shouts of joy from all parties echoed off the sides of the pyramid and surrounding mountains. When they subsided, they were followed by murmurs of confusion and concern.

"But where is this message?" someone called up. "We have not received it. Is it on its way?"

"We were afraid you would tell us that," Peter replied. "You see, that same bird, whom we now believe is a super heavenly spy, says that the message that the pope sent to all of you in Cholula was received by Commander Alvarado. Now hear this. The bird told us that your commander has decided that the pope's message goes against his best military judgment. He refuses to pass it on to you and has hidden it away in his clothes closet."

There was an awesome silence. Whispers and groans rose up from the courtyard. Finally, the vast majority of soldiers and Cholulans cried out, "Treason! The commander has no right to violate our right to freedom of religion!"

"We must rise up against him and strip him of his powers. The pope's message was sent to *us*! He has stolen it!" others cried.

At just that moment, Alvarado appeared. The children recognized him at once—the long, gaunt face, the bent nose and eyes that darted about suspiciously. He looked up at the children, shielding his eyes from the sun, and shouted to the officers.

"Who are these rabble-rousers inciting you to disobey my orders? Yes, I recognize them. They are the children who aided Montezuma with his cruelties. That was over twenty years ago, and they have not grown. Yes, they are devils who are being worshiped by these savages. Lieutenant Garcia, order the men under your command to seize them at once. Tie them up, gag them, and take them before a firing squad!"

Just then, the woman who was Alvarado's servant came running to the courtyard where the conquistadors stood. She was a pleasant-looking woman of thirty-five or so, dressed primly in her peasant blouse and long skirt but wearing no shoes on her feet as was the rule for all native women whose souls were nourished by contact with the earth. She was waving a scroll in her hand.

"Doña Lucia, what are you doing here?" Alvarado demanded of her.

"I didn't want to come, Senor Alvarado. But listening to these angels, whom you are threatening to kill, has forced me to speak out. The angels tell the truth! The pope has sent a message to you for the people, and you have hidden it in your closet so that no one would see it. I took it out when I heard the angels speak about the pope. I have it here in my hand. Do what you will to me!"

Alvarado tried to snatch it from her, but Lieutenant Francisco Juarez intercepted it.

"That can't be from the pope," Alvarado insisted. "You made it up, Doña Lucia!"

"Well, it's written in Spanish. Do you know Spanish, Doña Lucia?" Francisco asked her.

"I cannot read or write in Spanish or Nahuatl," the woman said. She was crying now. Many conquistadors crowded around the lieutenant as he unrolled the scroll.

"Listen to this," Lieutenant Juarez began. "The native people of America are not dumb brutes but human beings having souls!"

"And look at this!" Lieutenant Lopez read on. "They should all be welcomed into the folds of the church! And look here—this message is stamped with the holy seal of the Vatican!"

Lieutenant Juarez looked up at Sulma, who was standing with Peter and Rosa atop the mural of Quetzalcoatl. "Do you know what this means, Sulma?" he shouted. Sulma looked a little puzzled, as she had not understood all the words spoken in Spanish.

Rosa threw an arm around Sulma's waist. "It means you can marry Lieutenant Juarez!" Turning to the crowd below, Rosa cried out, "All of you—Spaniards, Cholulan women as well as Cholulan men—all of you are invited to marry in the church right up above us!" Wild cheers erupted throughout the crowd and beyond. People came running out of their houses to join the celebration. Spaniards and Cholulans danced together.

Lieutenant Lopez, Lieutenant Garcia, and Lieutenant Juarez addressed Commander Alvarado. "You, sir, are the one guilty of military misconduct by your lies and your orders that go against the laws of our nation and our service," Lieutenant Lopez declared.

Then Lieutenant Juarez spoke. "Fellow officers, let us appoint Lieutenant Lopez as our chief commander until we receive further notice from our commissioners in Tenochtitlan. In the meantime, we must arrest Commander Alvarado on the grounds of misusing his authority and imprison him in the military stockade until we receive further instructions."

The entire regiment of servicemen raised their arms and shouted in unison, "Hear! Hear! All hail the military forces of Charles V!" They continued to chant as Alvarado was seized and led away.

"And cheers to our angels who stand above us!"

Just then, Father Rodrigo arrived from his hiding place in the surrounding hills, saying he was ready to perform marriages.

"Can we begin tomorrow morning?" Lieutenant Juarez asked. "I think many other couples will also want to be wed. You will have a lot of work to do."

The young priest smiled. "I have fellow clergymen on their way."

Up on the mural, Sulma and the delegated angels applauded and began their descent to the courtyard.

Chapter 23

⁓

Peter and Rosa and Father Rodrigo spent the night with Francisco in his hacienda with a lovely garden courtyard and red-tiled roof. Sulma went off for her parent's home to prepare for her wedding. In the morning, they all met in Francisco's courtyard.

Two other clergymen, friends of Padre Rodrigo, arrived. They came with a beautiful white wedding gown decorated with flower and quetzal designs that had been embroidered by a Native American woman. The dress was presented to Sulma. She ran into one of the rooms to put it on. When she returned, everyone gasped. The gleaming white gown contrasted superbly with her smooth, reddish-brown skin and tumbling locks of rich, black hair.

A long line consisting of hundreds of couples waited outside to begin the ascent up the pyramid to the church that rested on its summit. The priests went up first. Peter and Rosa led the procession up the stairs. Sulma and Francisco followed behind them. Then came Lieutenant Lopez, smiling as he walked arm-in-arm with a young woman he'd had his eye on for some time. They were followed by Lieutenant "Beer Belly" Garcia, who had proposed to and been accepted by Lucia, Alvarado's former servant and later informer. When they reached the top of the pyramid, the line of betrothed couples stretched all the way down to the main square and beyond.

Peter and Rosa acted as best man and bridesmaid for Francisco and Sulma as well as their other friends.

The weddings went on all through the morning, afternoon, and early evening. Peter and Rosa stayed through the day to assist the priests in every way they could. Then, just as the sun was setting, the unthinkable happened, something that would have been considered a sacrilege only the day before. A bird flew into the church through the open doorway. Whispers rippled through the crowded pews as the winged creature, recognized by worshipers as a quetzal bird, came to rest on Rosa's shoulder. She was handing Padre Rodrigo a fresh bowl of communion wafers when the bird dropped a few soft coos into her ear. As quickly as it had come, the bird flew out of the church and was gone. After a stone silence, someone in the congregation was heard to say, "Surely, we have been visited by the Holy Spirit." Father Rodrigo bowed his head and said, "It is a sign that God has given his blessings to all of these weddings."

An hour later, the church closed and everybody started down the slope of the pyramid except Peter and Rosa. They watched the moon rise, casting a silver sheen over the great volcanoes. They were waiting because of what the quetzal bird had whispered in Rosa's ear—and then, yes, they saw the green, feathered serpent slither down a moon ray and land at their feet.

"Quetzalcoatl," the children cried joyfully, hugging the feathered coat. "You've come! Tell us. Is our job finished?"

The great god-serpent broke into a smile, exposing his saberlike teeth. "Yes, your job is finished. Mission accomplished! You have passed all your previous tests with flying colors, and now you've succeeded with the most difficult of them. You have laid the foundation for a new world, a world of freedom and equal opportunity for all. You have taken the first step in a struggle that will engage humankind for centuries. But for you, school is out. There will be no more tests, no more lessons from me. This is your graduation day. You are both well prepared to return to your world and times and take on whatever challenges come your way. I give you my congratulations and heartfelt blessings."

"Thank you so much. *Gracias, maestro!*" Rosa exclaimed.

"But—my father. What about my father?" Peter asked. "Will I finally learn who my father is?"

"Yes. It will be revealed to you soon. But now I must be off." The serpent looked down his feathered suit that was a code of time. "I have business among the stars."

"Before you go, *maestro*," Rosa said. "It's good that Peter will learn about his father, but besides that, if this is our graduation day, do we get a graduation present to take home, a reward of some kind?"

Quetzalcoatl nodded his great head thoughtfully. "Well now, how shall I put it? Yes. Take a good look at one another. Look deeply into each other's eyes. Think of all the things you've done in your travels together, how you've changed, and what you've finally found together. Yes, that thing you have found together is your reward."

Peter and Rosa looked at one another in astonishment, their faces reddening as they gasped for breath.

"And so, my children, I leave you with this quetzal feather and wish you a safe journey home. *Saludos, mis hijos!*" With that the plumed serpent was off, soaring into the night sky.

Peter and Rosa were left alone, staring at one another wordlessly, in the silence of the closed church atop the great pyramid.

Feeling the need to say something, Peter said, his voice creaking, "What do you think Quetzalcoatl meant by all those things he said about us?" He knew it was a dumb question as soon as it came out of his mouth.

"You don't know?" Rosa sounded a little hurt.

"I'm sorry, Rosa. I guess I do. It's just that—well, actually, I've been thinking. Since we've spent so much time preaching love and marriage, maybe we should take our own advice. Not right now—we're too young—but someday, maybe we can … I mean, will you marry me? Of course, our being grown-ups is a long way off. One of us—it won't be me—but you may change your mind before that time comes."

Rosa broke into a wide smile, and tears of joy flowed down her cheeks. "I won't change my mind, Peter. You can count on that. We've been together now for thousands of years, and we seem to get along better with each coil of time. I don't think my feelings for you will change in just a handful of years. If you want to know the truth, I've been crazy for you ever since you offered me a drink from your canteen back in Tollan I."

Peter felt his heart dance in his chest. He drew Rosa to him, and she threw her arms around his shoulders. "Oh, Rosa, you are fantastic. I'm a lot slower than you when it comes to catching on to my feelings or the feelings of others. But now I know what Quetzalcoatl means by that thing we've found together. It's love. I love you, Rosa, and I can't imagine a better reward for all that we've accomplished together."

"And I love you, Peter. Now maybe we can just have a taste of that reward."

Their lips met, and as they began to shiver together in ecstasy, everything spun around them and they zoomed off in cosmic space-time, racing with the speed of light.

Epilogue

~~~

Peter woke up to the smell of cooking coming from downstairs. Sunlight was streaming through his bedroom window. He looked at the clock on his dresser. It was seven thirty in the morning. He heard his mother talking with a man over the breakfast table. Peter groaned, recognizing the man's voice. It was the person he dreaded to see more than any other he had known. Yes, it was Ben, his stepfather, home from the hospital at last, just as his mother had promised the day before. Of course, for Peter, the day before seemed like years ago. But all the same, the time had come, and Peter would now have to confront the person who had caused most of the misery and humiliation he had ever known.

With this in mind, Peter roused himself, went to the bathroom to wash up, got dressed, and started down the stairs. As he descended, he told himself he would stand up to Ben, let him know he would never again tolerate his insults. Peter was no longer the confused, frightened little boy he had been just a few years ago. Thanks to Quetzalcoatl, he had learned that insulting remarks tend to be like those smoking mirrors that gave you a distorted image of yourself when you looked in them. And thanks to Quetzalcoatl, Peter had learned to direct his darts right at those mirrors, causing them to explode, engulfing their wearers in scorching fumes and making them run off screaming in agony and terror.

But for all Peter's resolve to confront Ben, his dread of his stepfather was in his bones. He approached the kitchen door shaking with the feeling he was about to face the greatest challenge of his life.

Peter entered the kitchen to see his mother, lovelier than ever and sitting in her bathrobe, golden locks piled on her head, while Ben sat across from her, his big, pointy ears protruding. Peter was surprised to see that Ben's outstanding beer belly had shrunk quite a bit.

Looking up at her son, Mrs. Collins broke into a smile. "There you are at last, sleepyhead." She waved a hand toward Ben. "Look! He's back. Your father—well, stepfather—Ben. He's back from the hospital to stay with us. Now we can be a family again. Isn't it wonderful?"

Peter stood frozen, giving his mother a startled look. She caught his reaction and went on. "Oh, I know you've had a few differences between you the last few years, but we now have the opportunity to become a happy family again."

Peter was aghast. What was she saying? A few differences between them? He and Ben? Why, his mother had herself found Ben's insults to him inexcusable and had said so in front of them both only two years ago. Now she was talking about their all becoming a happy family. He knew it was a dream of hers, but she had to know it was out of the question.

Again, Mrs. Collins was reading his mind. "I know what you're thinking, Peter, but a lot of things have changed for Ben and for me since he's been in the hospital. Remember, you stopped visiting him in the hospital over a year ago. A lot has changed since then, but I'll let Ben speak for himself."

Ben looked up and gave Peter a weary smile. "Good morning, Peter," he said with a gentle nod. "You can't imagine how much I've looked forward to seeing you again. I kept telling Doctor Feelgood how proud I am of you and of your many accomplishments in school and everything."

Peter was stupefied. Was this some kind of joke? Was it to be followed by a laugh of mockery or some vicious slur? But Ben was looking at him with a kind smile, speaking softly, respectfully. "I owe you a lot," he said. "First of all, I owe you an apology. I have not been a good father to you in the past several years. But I have learned a lot about myself in my two years at Back to Reality Hospital. I have learned about my stupidity, selfishness, my lack of tolerance and understanding. I beg your forgiveness for all the bad ways I acted toward you and hope to make up for them."

Ben looked down at the table quietly for a few seconds before going on. "First of all, I am sorry for the damage I may have done to your self-respect by all my insults to you, although I am amazed and delighted to see what a confident, brave, and strong young man you are becoming. But I know that something has been nagging at your soul for a long time. I have come to the conclusion that my failures as a father have caused you to become obsessed with wanting to know who your biological father is. You need an ideal to look up to, and I am not that ideal."

Ben looked over at Peter's mother, who had an anxious expression on her face. He took a sip of the coffee in front of him and went on. "Your mother can tell you that I am the chief obstacle to your knowing who your real father is. She hasn't revealed the truth to you in the past because she was afraid of offending me and spoiling my chances of being a father to you by telling you about the real one. But I think it is time to set things straight. Louise, this is where you come in. I want you to tell Peter about the man who fathered him."

"Ben, I'm not sure this is a good idea," Peter's mother put in, looking very upset. "I always wanted Peter to see you as his father and not get mixed up with the man from whom he inherited his genes. That man never saw Peter. It was only a short time after Peter was born that you and I married."

"Yes, we married because you wanted Peter to have a father. Well, I was a bad choice."

"Ben, let's not talk about that now. Let's talk about the future. You're a changed man, a good man, the man I knew before all that business in Mexico happened."

"Mexico?" Peter was stunned. Yes, Mexico! He always had believed some part of him was Mexican. And why had Quetzalcoatl, a Mexican god, singled him out in the first place? Peter was thrilled to think that the secret that had eluded him all his life was at last going to be revealed to him.

"We must go back to what happened in Mexico. That's the only way we can go forward from here," Ben said. He turned to Peter. "Son, I have to tell you that for all the macho talk you've heard from me over the years, I was a wimp when I first knew your mother. You see, we went to Mexico together shortly before you were born. It was like a honeymoon before the wedding, a way of seeing if we could really get along. Your mother had taken a course in Mexican archaeology in college, and she wanted to see the pyramids outside Mexico City and then go into the jungle in the Yucatan. She was a real tripper, your mother. As for me, I wimped out trying to climb one of those big pyramids. I think they called it the Pyramid of the Sun. I got a third of the way up, and your mother had to help me down. Later, when she said, 'Let's go to Chiapas and visit the rain forest,' I panicked. It was the time when those masked rebels with guns had taken over a lot of places in that rain forest. I figured that with my redneck, gringo looks, I'd be dead meat for them. Your mother, on the other hand, was a real looker, as she is today, and I knew they would love her up. It was the biggest mistake I ever made. I lent your mother some money, enough to hire a guide and for things they'd need, and told her I would wait for her in a hotel in Mexico City. I chose a Hilton of all places. Well, she went off, and when she came back six weeks later, you were inside her tummy."

"Ben, the way you put it!"

"All right, Louise. You put it the way you want to. It's your story. Tell Peter and me how you became a Zapatista bride."

Louise blushed like a little girl, something Peter had never seen her do. "Well, yes," she said. "It all happened after the Zapatista uprising that began on New Year's Eve of 1994. That's when a band of rebels wearing ski masks and carrying rifles took over the City Hall in San

Cristobal de las Casas. Las Casas is located high in the mountains of the state of Chiapas, the southernmost state in Mexico."

Louise took a long sip of coffee before going on. "The Zapatistas had come to Chiapas to fight for the rights of Mayan peasants who had been uprooted from their homes in the highlands by greedy landowners. The landowners had bands of armed men who drove the peasants from the land that had been theirs for generations." Louise shrugged and sighed heavily. "Well, the Mexican government could not or did not control the landowners, but it did drive the Zapatistas out of San Cristobal. It wasn't long before the Zapatistas took their crusade to the Lacandon rain forest where the persecuted peasants had fled to find new homes. Not being satisfied with driving them out of the highlands, the landowners wanted to rout the Mayan peasants from their jungle refuge. I saw it happen firsthand."

Louise poured herself and the others more coffee. "I'd always been interested in the struggle of the Mayans and other native groups, so I hired an experienced guide, as Ben said, and he took me to the small jungle town of El Capulin. There was an old church, the ruins of an ancient Mayan temple, a lot of mud adobe houses with straw roofs, and some of the nicest people I have ever met." She paused to smile at the memory.

Then her expression quickly changed to one of grief. "I didn't know that something terrible was soon going to happen to them and me. I was happy to meet them, and they all saw me as somebody special. I was a young American woman with light blonde hair and blue eyes, someone the likes of which they had never seen." And here she paused with a small smile and a faint blush on her cheeks. "They saw me as a fit partner for their new leader, who was himself regarded as someone very special. That's putting it mildly. He was a Zapatista whom they revered as a god. I was soon introduced to Zapatista Topiltzin, whom they all hailed as an incarnation of the god Quetzalcoatl, one of the most important gods in the Mayan religion. You know of him, don't you, Peter?"

"Yes, I—uh, Rosa and I have been studying ancient Mexican religions. You know, of course, that Quetzalcoatl was called Kulkulan by the Maya." Peter was stunned by what his mother was saying and waited with baited breath for her to continue.

"Exactly. Good for you, Peter. Of course, *you* know what incarnation means. For the people of El Capulin, Zapatista Topiltzin was the feathered serpent god given human form. Indeed, he wore a helmet from which a band of quetzal feathers trailed, just like the feather you found in your bed a few years ago, Peter."

Peter looked at his mother intently. "You say his name was Topiltzin and you met him! Just what happened between you?" Peter was breathing hard now, and his hands trembled with excitement.

Louise paused as if unsure whether to continue her story, but Ben egged her on. "Tell us, Louise."

"Well, what can I say? He courted me. We all had a big dinner of roasted pheasant. Afterward, he led me off to drink some steaming chocolate under a ceiba tree. Then he removed his mask, and I was enchanted. It was not so much that he was handsome. No reflection on you, Ben. You were handsome in those days, and to me you still are. But the way he looked at me, the very way he carried himself—Zapatista Topiltzin was godlike, a divine presence. Yes, it was as if God's grace flowed through his entire being. So when he asked me to marry him—I don't know. I was young and so enchanted, I consented. It may not have been fair to Ben, but I was swept off my feet."

She paused as if savoring the memory of the proposal and her acceptance. When she went on, her expression turned to sadness. "It wasn't an official wedding, not one that would be accepted in America or even in other parts of Mexico. It was the kind of wedding that was common for the people of El Capulin and other Mayan groups living in the jungle. It was held in a Catholic church but performed by a shaman, a priest of the Maya. It was a wedding in which the married couple received the blessings not only of the Christian God and the Blessed Virgin but of all of the gods of the Maya. It was believed that the spirits of the Mayan gods were hidden inside the statues of the saints that lined the walls of the church."

Suddenly, tears rolled down Louise's cheeks. Peter had never seen his mother cry before.

"Yes, the wedding in the Church of the Virgin was joyous. But within a month, that church was the scene of a great tragedy for me and for so many others. As I told you, the rich landowners in the hills had come down into the jungle to take the Mayan peasants' new homes away from them. And they set out to murder all those who got in their way. They also had plans to destroy the rain forest and create new farmland where ceiba trees had stood for thousands of years.

"So only two Sundays after our wedding, a militia serving the rich landowners and armed with AK-47 rifles and pistols stormed the church, killing first of all my husband, who protected me with his body just before he fell. Then they killed dozens of men, women, and children."

Louise could hardly go on. She was sobbing now, her voice choking. She rested one arm on Ben's shoulder and clasped Peter's hand with the other. "And so my life was spared, thanks to Topiltzin giving up his own to save me and to save you, Peter. When I left El Capulin and returned to Ben in Mexico City, you were growing inside me. And thank God for Ben, to whom I told all the details of this story. Ben offered to marry me and help me raise another man's child."

"I haven't been a good father to you," Ben said now. "But I'm going to make up for all that, you'll see. Please forgive my stupidity in telling you time and time again that you weren't born with the right stuff. I was just jealous. From everything I know, your father was a wonderful guy."

Louise nodded, and a faint smile came to her face. "Yes, he was wonderful, and from a Mayan point of view, he was a god. Peter, if Topiltzin Zapata was one of the incarnations of Quetzalcoatl, then you are Quetzalcoatl's son. If you remember, I had a dream a few years ago in which Quetzalcoatl appeared to me and told me he was helping you grow up to be a brave, good person that we would all be proud of. Yes, he is your father."

Peter was astounded. "Of course. It all makes sense—the visits of the serpent in the middle of the night, the travels, the training, the building of my confidence, all the advice." Peter wept with joy as tears streamed down his cheeks.

As they did, a look of concern came over his mother's face. "But, Peter, for all of that, I want you to remember that Ben has tried his very best to be a father to you, despite the mistakes he has made in the past few years. He was good to you when you were little. And all the things we have—this house, the way we live—are all thanks to Ben."

Ben smiled, but there was sadness in his eyes. "Yes, Peter, I'm proud of you. For all the mistakes I've made in being a father to you, from now on I'll always be at your side, helping you in every way I can."

Peter looked at his mother and then at Ben in wonder. He shook his head and opened his hands wide. "You know, all my life I wanted to know who my father was. I often felt I didn't really have one. And now I know that I have two fathers."

They all got up from the breakfast table, laughing and hugging one another.

On his way to school that morning, Peter ran into Rosa as he turned down a tree-lined street. He told her he had just learned from his mother that his father was Quetzalcoatl himself. Rosa hooted with joy.

"That means when we get married, Quetzalcoatl will be my father-in-law," Rosa said with a big smile.

They laughed together. "Oh, Rosa, I can't wait. And, funny, the way you look now, you remind me of somebody, some great beauty I might have known in the past, but I can't remember who it is."

Rosa went into gales of laughter. "Peter, I think I know who it is. My aunt bought a computer, and my brother is teaching her how to use it. My aunt always wanted to know who our ancestors were, going way back in time. My brother said there was a way of searching for ancestors on the Internet, and they discovered the name of the first of my aunts who had an ancient Mexican first name and a Spanish last name. Do you know who it was?"

"No, how would I know?" Peter asked.

"Because you knew her. Her name is Sulma Juarez."

"Sulma Juarez?"

Rosa laughed. "Yes, the woman who went with us to the top of the mural in Cholula and later married Lieutenant Francisco Juarez in the Church of La Virgen de los Remedios."

Peter was thunderstruck. "Sulma Juarez! Good God, she was absolutely lovely. And you are growing up to be just like her! I can't wait."

"It's only a few years from now. Peter, I waited for you a thousand years, remember?"

They laughed together and continued down the tree-lined street, arm in arm, Rosa's head resting on Peter's shoulder.